"Shaye!"

"Cole?"

Her voice was weak, but relief hit him hard, a wave that almost took him to his knees. She was alive.

He rounded the second car and found her huddled near the back tire. The flat back tire, Cole realized. The gunman's final shot must have just missed her.

But relief was short-lived, because she was hit. There was a trail of blood alongside the car, as if she'd dragged herself here. He yanked his cell phone out, calling Monica directly. "Gunman ran east out of Roy's parking lot, on foot. Male, white, average height and build, wearing jeans and a dark hoodie, carrying at least one pistol. Send backup. And get me an ambulance to Roy's, right now."

He barely paused as he knelt next to Shaye, who was abnormally pale, her freckles standing out more than usual against her porcelain skin, her red hair tangled around her face and her pretty brown eyes huge. "Talk to me. Are you okay?"

Police Protector

ELIZABETH HEITER

MILLS & BOON

First Published in Great Britain 2017
By Mills & Boon, an imprint of HarperCollins*Publishers*
1 London Bridge Street, London, SE1 9GF

Large Print edition 2017

© 2017 Elizabeth Heiter

ISBN: 978-0-263-07238-9

Our policy is to use papers that are natural, renewable and recyclable products and made from wood grown in sustainable forests. The logging and manufacturing processes conform to the legal environmental regulations of the country of origin.

Printed and bound in Great Britain
by CPI Antony Rowe, Chippenham, Wiltshire

Elizabeth Heiter likes her suspense to feature strong heroines, chilling villains, psychological twists and a little romance. Her research has taken her into the minds of serial killers, through murder investigations and onto the FBI Academy's shooting range. Elizabeth graduated from the University of Michigan with a degree in English literature. She's a member of International Thriller Writers and Romance Writers of America. Visit Elizabeth at www.elizabethheiter.com.

It's amazing to have friends who've been by your side since childhood. Robbie Terman, Jaime Pulliam, Julie Gabe and Esi Akaah— this one's for you!

Acknowledgements

Thank you to Paula Eykelhof, Kayla King, Denise Zaza and everyone involved in bringing *Police Protector* to readers. Thanks to my family and friends for their endless support, especially my "usual suspects": Kevan Lyon, Chris Heiter, Robbie Terman, Andrew Gulli, Kathryn Merhar, Caroline Heiter, Kristen Kobet, Ann Forsaith, Charles Shipps, Sasha Orr, Nora Smith and Mark Nalbach.

Chapter One

She'd made it.

Shaye Mallory smiled as she juggled two bags of groceries and headed toward her ten-year-old sedan at the far end of the grocery store parking lot. She'd been back to work at Maryland's Jannis County forensics lab for a full week now.

A full week where no one had shot at her.

It felt like a good reason for a celebration, so tonight's trip to the grocery store had included a big carton of chocolate-chunk ice cream. She tried not to feel too pathetic that she'd be having that celebration all by herself on a Friday night in her living room with an old movie and spoonful after spoonful of sugar.

But she'd lived in Maryland for only two years. She'd moved out here for the computer specialist job. She worked with police officers in her role, but bullets had seemed as foreign to her as living alone, far away from her big family. When she'd left the forensics lab last year after the shooting, most of those friendships had eventually lapsed. At the job she'd taken in tech support before returning to the lab, she'd kept mostly to herself. Although she had friends, there wasn't anyone close enough to tell she wanted to celebrate going a week without being shot at or having a nervous breakdown. And celebrating with her family over video chat seemed way too pathetic, not to mention that it would get them worried about her all over again.

The truth was today was a milestone for her. A year ago, when she'd quit the job, she'd sworn she'd never return. Never walk back into the forensics lab parking lot—one that was shared with the Jannis City Police Department—where she'd watched three officers die. Where she'd hit the pavement, panicking as shots rang out, having no way to defend herself, knowing she was going to be next.

The shiver of fear that bolted up her spine now was just a memory, Shaye told herself, repositioning her bags so she could dig out her car key. She'd worked late tonight, but when she'd arrived at the store, the parking lot had been relatively full. Apparently she'd spent too long inside debating treats because now it was nearly empty. She forced herself not to spin around, not to check her surroundings, not to give in to the paranoia that had caused her more than one moment of embarrassment over the past week.

But she'd done it. She'd conquered her fear and finally called the forensics lab back, finally accepted their offers to return to her old job.

Every single time she'd walked into the parking lot where the shooting had happened, she'd felt a near-paralyzing fear. She'd frozen more than once before stepping out of her car, but she'd done it. And each day she'd paused for slightly less time before gathering the courage to run for the lab.

But everything was getting back to normal now, Shaye reminded herself. Soon—hopefully—she'd hardly even remember feeling afraid.

If only she could say that right now. She stopped ignoring the tingle at the back of her neck and glanced around the vacant lot, dimly lit with bulbs and two cars, barely keeping hold of her groceries as she slid her key into her door. She swore as one of the bags ripped and started sliding out of her hands.

She dropped to her knees, trying to catch the

bag before eggs broke everywhere, and then a *boom* she'd recognize anywhere rang out. A gunshot.

She panicked, and her feet slid out from underneath her, sending groceries smashing to the ground. Then another gunshot split the night air, and pain exploded in her hip.

Dropping lower to the ground, Shaye looked around the parking lot, certain she'd see that same rusted-out sedan with the spinning rims from a year ago cruising to a stop, gang members leaning out the windows with semi-automatics. Instead she saw a lone figure running across the dark parking lot toward her, a weapon in his hands.

Shaye whimpered, her blood racing through her veins so fast her whole body started to shake as blood spread on the leg of her khakis. *Not again.* And this time she was all alone. No Cole Walker, heroic police detective and star in too many of her fantasies, to save her.

Fear overrode her ability to think clearly as her brain went back to that horrible evening when gang members had tried to get revenge on the police station for investigating them. She'd been dawdling as she'd left the lab, hanging out closer to the station than her own building, hoping for a chance to run into Cole, when the gunfire started. Shoving the memories back, she glanced up at the key in her car door. Could she get it unlocked, get inside and start the car fast enough?

She looked back toward the shooter, who'd made it halfway to her and stopped to line up another shot through the lot's dim lighting.

Pressing her feet hard against the concrete, Shaye launched herself toward the front of her car. She heard another bullet hit—probably her car—but didn't stop to check.

Adrenaline pumped so hard she couldn't feel the bullet wound on her leg, or the nasty scrapes she knew she'd made on her hands and knees when she'd shoved herself along the concrete. She kept going, her heart thudding in her eardrums as she scurried around to the other side of her car. It wouldn't be a barrier for long, but now he'd have to get closer to hit her.

There was another car ten feet away. If she could make a run for it, dart for new cover while he was trying to move closer, maybe it would give someone inside time to call the police. Or another vehicle would pull into the lot and scare him off. She scrambled to her knees and got ready to race for the other car, but the sound of footsteps pounded toward her too quickly, and she knew she'd never make it in time.

A sob lodged in her throat as she readied herself to make a run for it anyway, one last desperate effort to survive when she knew she was going to fail. She'd lived through the shooting at the lab, actually conquered her fears enough to return to that job, and now she was going to die in a supermarket parking lot.

"SHOTS FIRED AT Roy's Grocery."

The call came in over his radio, and Cole Walker scowled at it, then pressed the button and replied. "Detective Walker. I'm a minute out. Responding."

He punched the gas as Monica's voice came back to him, "Aren't you off duty, Detective?"

It was a rhetorical question, so he didn't bother answering. A cop was never really off duty.

"We believe there's a single gunman in the parking lot," Monica advised him. "Call came in from the owner, who thinks there's at least one customer out there, too. No other information at this time."

"Got it," he muttered, not bothering to key the radio. It didn't really matter what information they had; with shots fired, they always reacted as though there could be more gunmen. Ever since the shooting at the station last year, calls about gunfire spurred extra caution.

That thought instantly made an image of Shaye Mallory form in his head. He wouldn't have been anywhere near Roy's Grocery, except he'd been on his way—uninvited—to her house. And the store was only a few miles down the road from her. His gaze caught on the champagne bottle with a ribbon on it that rolled off his seat and smacked the floor as he whipped his truck into the grocery store parking lot.

The store had crappy lighting, but he zoned in on the shooter immediately. The man glanced back at him, a hoodie obscuring his face, and then darted around one of two cars in the lot, firing at something—or someone—behind it before sprinting around the corner.

Cole hit the gas, scanning the parking lot for any sign of additional shooters. But he saw no one as he raced past the first car. He was ready to continue past the second after the shooter when his mind registered the make and model of the first one—he recognized it. He slammed on the brakes, yanked his truck into Park and had his weapon out of its holster before he'd even cleared the door.

"Shaye!"

"Cole?"

Her voice was weak, but relief hit him hard, a wave that almost took him to his knees. She was alive.

He rounded the second car and found her huddled near the back tire. The *flat* back tire, Cole realized. The gunman's final shot must have just missed her.

But relief was short-lived because she was hit. There was a trail of blood alongside the car, as if she'd dragged herself here. He yanked his cell phone out, calling Monica directly. "Gunman ran east out of Roy's parking lot on foot.

Male, white, average height and build, wearing jeans and a dark hoodie, carrying at least one pistol. Send backup. And get me an ambulance to Roy's right now."

He barely paused as he knelt next to Shaye, who was abnormally pale, her freckles standing out more than usual against her porcelain skin, her red hair tangled around her face and her pretty brown eyes huge. "Talk to me. Are you okay?"

He didn't wait for an answer, but tucked his phone against his shoulder, holstered his weapon and found the source of all that blood. It was coming from her right leg, up near her hip. Finding where the bullet had entered, he grabbed the fabric of her khakis and ripped so he could see the wound.

"Hey," she complained, but her voice was even weaker, and she leaned her head against the car as he prodded carefully around her wound.

It was bleeding badly, but not as badly as it would have been if the shooter had gotten a major artery. He slid his hand down into the leg of her pants around to the back of her thigh and found what he suspected. An exit wound. The bullet had gone straight through.

"How bad is it?" Shaye whispered, her eyelids dropping to half-mast.

"You're going to be fine," he promised.

"What's happening?" Monica asked in his ear. "Backup is close. Two minutes out."

He cursed inwardly, hoping the shooter wouldn't be long gone before officers arrived. Two minutes was too long. This guy had shot Shaye. Cole wanted him in handcuffs now.

Monica's voice sounded in his ear again. "I'm getting that ambulance now."

"Cancel it." Cole shifted his weight and warned Shaye, "This might hurt a little." Then he wiped the blood on his hands onto the leg of his pants and scooped her into his arms. "Shaye Mallory was hit," he said into his phone as Shaye's arms went around his neck and she tucked her head against his chest, almost before he saw her wince with pain and clamp her jaw closed.

"I'm driving her to the hospital myself," he told Monica as he hurried back to his truck, deposited her in the passenger seat and then ran around to the driver's side. "I'll call you when we get there. Send me updates as they come in," he said, then hung up the phone and hopped in the truck, yanking it back into Drive.

As he sped out of the parking lot, Shaye asked, "Were you on your way to a date?"

"What?" He frowned over at her, both at the oddity of her question and the way her voice sounded like she was in a daze.

She gestured to her feet, and he looked down, realizing she was talking about the bottle of champagne on his floorboard, which was still miraculously unbroken.

"That was for you," he replied, seeing her confusion before he yanked his attention back onto the road and drove as fast as he could through the surface streets toward the freeway.

"For me?"

"Put pressure on your wound," he said, instead of explaining that he'd gotten it to celebrate her returning to work.

He risked a glance at her as her head dropped forward. As if she'd just realized how much blood there was, she pressed both hands down frantically against her leg.

She was coming out of her shock. He'd seen enough shooting victims to know what was coming next: panic.

He tried to stave it off as he merged onto the freeway and punched it up to ninety. "We'll be at the hospital in three minutes," he promised, keeping his tone calm despite the fear he felt. "You're fine. It's a flesh wound. I know it looks like a lot, but the bullet went through and you haven't lost enough blood for it to be a problem."

He'd seen enough bullet wounds to know when they were life threatening. But he'd also seen enough to know that sometimes they surprised you. He'd seen people operate on adrenaline, actually getting up and running, when their injuries said they should already be dead. And he'd seen minor wounds turn fatal.

Not for Shaye, he promised himself, speeding off the freeway. A few more too-fast turns and then he made an illegal turn into the hospital parking lot and slammed to a stop. He tossed his key at the valet and ran around the other side to open Shaye's door.

An orderly was coming their way with a wheelchair, but Cole ignored him, reaching in to lift Shaye himself. If it was possible, she looked even more pale and terrified, reminding him of that day almost exactly a year ago and the drive-by at the station. Shaye had been caught in the middle of it all.

"Why does this keep happening?" she whispered, then promptly passed out.

Chapter Two

Shaye woke in a hospital bed, a warm blanket pulled up to her chin and a frowning nurse strapping a blood pressure cuff to her arm.

"How are you feeling?"

She'd recognize that voice anywhere. Shaye turned her head, and there was Cole, perched at the edge of a chair next to her bed, his reddish-blond hair rumpled and concern etched onto his normally laid-back expression.

Embarrassment heated her. Had she actually *fainted*?

Okay, yes, she was a lab rat, and gun battles—except for the gang shooting that still gave her nightmares—were *way* outside her experience. But she'd managed to make a run for that second car, hiding until Cole had magically arrived. She'd managed to stay relatively cool until they'd made it safely to the hospital.

Yet she'd fainted in front of Jannis's best detective, the guy who'd led the charge to bring down the entire gang's network after that shooting. Cole was one of the bravest people she knew.

And she was most definitely not.

"I'm okay," she said, surprised when her voice came out weak. She realized just how tired she was.

"We stitched up your wound," the nurse told her, jotting something down and then taking the blood pressure cuff off her arm. "You were lucky—it went straight through and didn't hit anything crucial. The doctor is going to want to watch your vitals for a few hours, but then we'll send you home. You should be feeling fine in a few days."

Shaye nodded, trying not to focus on the dread she'd felt as soon as the nurse mentioned leaving the hospital. Would she ever feel safe again? Or would everywhere she went become like the forensics lab, requiring her to psyche herself up to leave her house? Tears welled, and she shoved them back, refusing to show any more weakness in front of Cole.

Once she knew no tears were going to escape, she looked over at him, hopeful. "Did they get the shooter?"

He frowned, shaking his head. "Not yet. But we're already reaching out to the news stations. We'll be putting out a call for information on all the evening shows. Someone will know something. We'll find him."

She shivered, suddenly cold, pulling the blanket tighter around her. Would they really? The department was good. She'd seen firsthand how dedicated they were. But with nothing to go on but a vague description of a gunman? Especially one who'd managed to escape the police's net?

Cole must have sensed the direction of her thoughts, because he said, "We've got officers at the scene now, pulling the slugs from your car. The security camera at the grocery store was just for show, but we're canvassing the area, hoping someone saw the shooter running away. And we're checking nearby traffic cameras, too. Unless he lives close by, he must have had a vehicle waiting. Once we find that, it's over."

There was a dark determination to his voice that told her he planned to be there to slap on the handcuffs himself.

And what he was saying made sense. Although her job was peripheral—she analyzed digital devices like laptops or cell phones that cops brought to her under the fluorescent lights in her lab—she'd seen how investigations worked.

Roy's Grocery was in a safe area. There were a lot of independent businesses there, and it was close to family neighborhoods. People watched out for one another. They would report someone running away after hearing gunshots. Logically, that would lead to a location where the shooter had a car waiting, and a license plate they could run through their system to get a name. She'd seen it happen before. She'd seen it work plenty of times.

But she'd also helped with cases where they'd come up empty no matter how hard they tried, and she couldn't shake the feeling that this was going to be one of those cases. Even worse, she hadn't been any help at all. All she could say about the shooter was that he was male, probably white, definitely determined to kill her.

"Do you think it was the same people from last year?" She spoke her deepest fear.

Gangs didn't give up. They didn't forgive, and they held grudges.

The police had rounded up the whole group, killing some at the scene, then getting the driver from her identification. After that, they'd worked tirelessly to bring down the leadership, being creative by going after them on racketeering charges, using the digital trail she'd found before the shooting, before she'd quit. But was everyone behind bars, or had they missed someone? Had someone gotten out?

With gangs anything was possible, including someone new making a play to bring the group back, to make a name for himself by taking out the key witness in the trial that had brought down the old leadership. Last year she'd worried that she'd never be safe again. There had actually been talk of the Witness Protection Program.

But Cole and his partner had kept at it, even working with local FBI agents in one of the biggest task forces their small department had ever seen. She'd been gone by then, but she'd heard the rumors. Cole had ignored death threats. He'd kept going until he was certain every member was behind bars.

She'd seen the news headlines later that year, too, proclaiming the demise of the Jannis Crew gang. Her fear of returning to the station hadn't gone away, but at the time, her logical brain had said there was no more reason for her to be scared.

"We're looking into it," Cole said, fury in the hard lines of his jaw. "But don't worry. Chances are this is totally unrelated. You were probably a random victim, just in the wrong parking lot when he happened to be looking for trouble."

"You think this guy was planning a mass shooting and the parking lot was emptier than he expected?" she asked. Or had Cole arrived before the shooter could head into the building to find more victims, she wondered, staring at the man who'd saved her life for the second time.

She flashed back to that moment when she'd flattened herself to the ground in a different parking lot, certain she was going to be killed. Back then, there'd been three other men in the lot with her, armed men, who'd each taken a bullet before they could unholster their weapons. She'd gotten as low as she could, with nowhere to run, bullets spraying over her head, and then Cole had run out the front door of the station, right into the line of fire.

"It's definitely a possibility," Cole said, and she refocused on their conversation.

Mass shooting. This was different from last year, she reminded herself. Except back then, she hadn't been an intended target, either. Just at the wrong place at the wrong time. How many chances would she get before she ran out of them, or Cole wasn't around to save her?

A shiver worked through her, and she spoke quickly to change the subject, knowing he'd seen it. "How long have I been here?"

He didn't even glance at his watch. "A few hours."

And he'd stayed beside her the whole time? She didn't need to ask. She could tell from the way the nurse had maneuvered around him when she'd left the room without even looking, as if she'd been doing it repeatedly.

She had an instant flashback to the day she'd arrived in Jannis, having accepted the job as a digital forensics examiner. She'd walked through the station doors, thinking it was connected to the laboratory she was supposed to report to, her palms slick with nerves and her stride quick with anticipation. She'd turned the corner toward security and walked smack into Cole Walker.

She was tall, and in the heels she'd worn that first day with her carefully tailored suit, she'd been close to his six feet. But even in heels, she didn't have slow or dainty strides. She walked with purpose, so she'd collided with him hard. Enough that the impact with his rock-hard chest had almost sent her to the ground.

The memory made her flush, warming her up, and Cole's lips turned up at the corners like he could tell what she was thinking. Before he could comment on it, she blurted, "I'm not quitting."

He looked surprised by her outburst, and, in truth, it had surprised her, too. She'd had no idea she was even thinking it until the words came out, but as soon as she spoke, she realized they were true.

A year ago she'd let the tragedy at the station derail her career. The fact was she'd let it derail her life.

She was scared. But how many times could she be this unlucky?

And she was tired of running from the things that scared her. She met Cole's gaze, momentarily distracted by the perfect sky blue of his eyes, then felt her shoulders square on the scratchy hospital pillow. "Whatever needs to be done to catch this guy, I want to be a part of it."

HAPPINESS BURST FORTH, then instantly warred with Cole's need to keep Shaye safe.

He'd been thrilled when she had returned to the lab. It had been part of his motivation when he'd called her a month ago, asking for some off-the-books help with a situation his foster brother Andre had been battling. When she'd provided key information to help them nail the guy who'd been coming after his brother's new girlfriend, he'd seen it boost her confidence again. Even more, he'd seen it remind her how much she loved the electronic chase.

He'd worked with enough forensics specialists in his years at the police department to know Shaye was special. She had a gift with computers, able to pull from them things no one else could find. And that kind of talent rarely came without passion.

When she'd left the job last year, he'd understood. A tiny part of him had even been glad, because it kept her out of the line of fire while they chased down the dangerous gang nervy enough to stage a drive-by at a police station. But he'd missed seeing her every day, those few moments each morning when they'd walk in from the parking lot together before she veered off to the county's forensics lab located behind the station. Those few moments each evening when she'd wait for him outside the station doors, and they'd stand and chat before going their separate ways.

Once he'd been confident they'd shut the gang down, he'd reached out a few times, tried to convince Shaye to return. He knew her director had, too. But each time she'd refused, seeming embarrassed by the fact that she was afraid to come under fire again. So he was shocked that she was standing her ground now.

"Are you sure?" he asked. Before she could argue, he continued. "Believe me—I want you to stay. I think this is where you belong. But we don't know who came after you today— and although I don't think you were the target, I want to be sure. Your safety is most important."

"I—"

"Hopefully, we'll catch him today and discover he's acting alone and picked you at random. But until we're certain, I think you should go into protective custody."

When she looked ready to argue, he held up a hand. "Not WitSec. I'm not asking you to give up your life here. This is nothing like last year."

He hoped that was true. Nothing about this

situation resembled the other—the shooter hadn't been wearing gang colors, and he'd gone after Shaye at a store, instead of attacking where the rest of the gang's presumed targets would be, back at the station. All logic pointed to this being random.

But he couldn't shake the fear that someone wanted Shaye dead. And he couldn't let anything happen to her.

"Just temporary police protection," he continued, trying to stop his morose thinking. "Then, once we're sure you're out of danger, you get back to work." He reached out and took her hand, which felt cold and tiny on top of the too-warm blanket. "Deal?"

"No."

He almost laughed at the stubborn tilt of her chin, the petulant look in her eyes. But this wasn't a joking matter. "No?" he repeated, in his best "bad cop" voice.

Staring at her now, looking so vulnerable in

that hospital bed, made all his protective instincts fire to life. She might have belonged in forensics, but she could have gotten a job doing that anywhere. He'd been the one who'd lured her back to this department after she'd helped with his brother's case. So everything that was happening to her now was on him.

The idea that he'd had any part, no matter how small, in putting her back in danger left a sour taste in his mouth. He'd always been drawn to Shaye, from that first day she'd shown up at the station, looking nervous behind her determined posture.

She'd slammed into him, all lean muscle and surprisingly soft curves, and then her cheeks had gone such a deep red, he'd been immediately charmed. He'd sought out excuses to see her every day. But he'd never been able to bring himself to ask her out. She was shy and sweet and smart. She came from a close-knit family and he knew when she looked into her future, she saw someone solid and stable to share it with, someone with a normal job. She deserved far better than he'd ever be able to give her.

But when it came to this—when it came to her safety—he knew he was the best man for the job.

He could tell she was scared. It was there, behind the determination in her eyes, in the slight tremor in her hand. But she shook her head.

"I let a shooting scare me off once. I work in law enforcement. Maybe I'm just a lab rat and not a cop, but I'm not letting it force me out again."

"There's no shame in going into hiding for a short time," he told her, but she was already shaking her head again. "You know they'll hold your job for you."

"It doesn't matter." A smile quivered on her lips, fleeting and self-deprecating. "If I leave now, I'll never come back. And I want to do this job. I want this life. I'm not giving up on it."

Cole stared at her, not really sure what she meant by *this life*. But he could see it in her gaze—she wasn't going to back down. Which meant he'd have to keep her safe. It would be way more challenging than if she'd agree to go off the grid, but the more he thought about it, there were upsides, too.

With no evidence this was a targeted hit, he'd be hard-pressed to convince the brass to use resources to protect her. He knew he could talk them into it for a short time, but it wouldn't be easy. And if she went to a safe house, they'd assign a couple of patrol officers to watch her. If she kept working, he'd be on the case. He'd make sure of it. And that meant he'd also be personally in charge of her safety.

"Okay," he said, not pulling his hand away from hers even as her cheeks started to flush from the extended contact. "Have it your way.

But you'd better get used to having me around, then, because I'm not letting you out of my sight until we catch this guy."

Chapter Three

He wasn't letting her out of his sight?

All sorts of inappropriate thoughts ran through Shaye's mind until she was sure Cole could see exactly what she was thinking, especially when his pupils dilated, staring back at her.

She dropped her gaze to her lap, her heart thudding way too hard after the day she'd had, and pulled her hand free from his. She'd had a massive crush on Cole from the moment she'd met him. But if she hadn't already known it, last year's shooting had quickly shown her that they'd never work. While she'd turned in her resignation the very next morning—over the phone because she was too afraid to return to the scene of the crime—he'd gone right back to work.

They would never be equals. He would always be the brave detective with the badge and the gun, and here she was again, the terrified forensics expert. It couldn't be more obvious, with her stuck in this hospital bed, in a hospital gown someone had changed her into—she hoped not in front of Cole—and him ready to dive right into solving the case.

But this time would be different, she vowed. Because she might be way too shy, way too awkward, way too boring for a man like Cole Walker, but she was tired of feeling like a coward. Two years ago she'd moved out to Maryland from Michigan, leaving behind her big, well-meaning family and the anonymity that came with being the middle child in a group of five. She'd dived into the unfamiliar, trying to break out of her comfort zone. She'd even bought a house, putting down roots right away, to force herself to stay if things got tough. And things had sure gotten tough.

She wasn't going to let herself be driven out of the job she loved and the place she'd come to consider home a second time.

She clenched her jaw and looked back up at Cole, praying her cheeks would cool. "What do we know so far about the forensics? What can I do?"

Her specialty was computers, but she had plenty of cross-training. There had to be some way she could help catch this guy. And once they caught him, maybe she could get back to the task of putting her life back on track.

Cole patted her hand. "Right now I just want you to focus on healing up."

"I'm fine." She knew he didn't mean to condescend to her, but if she wanted him to take her seriously as a professional—and not a victim he had to take care of—she needed to show him a reason. She shoved off the blanket and got to her feet, remembering too late she was hooked up to an IV.

The nurse ran in as her monitor went off, and Shaye clapped her hand over the crook of her elbow where she'd pulled out the line.

Cole stood, tried to steady her as she wobbled a little on her feet. "What are you doing?"

"Going home."

"You need to be under observation," the nurse stated, scowling as she slapped a piece of cotton over the blood on Shaye's arm and taped it down.

"I'm fine," Shaye said. "The wound on my leg is closed, right? My heart rate and blood pressure have been pretty normal the whole time I've been in here." She'd been peeking over at her monitor periodically as she and Cole talked. "You said you were going to release me today. I'm ready to go."

The nurse frowned at her, but it was nothing compared with Cole's expression, a mixture of worry, frustration and anger.

Shaye stood her ground. "Have the doctor look at me if you need to, but I feel okay. I want to go home."

The nurse muttered something under her breath, then looked her over. "All right. But if you start feeling dizzy or your wound opens up, I want you to come back here—understood?"

Nodding, Shaye hoped she wasn't making a mistake. But she couldn't stay here any longer. She needed answers about who had shot at her—and why. And she wasn't going to get them on her back in a hospital bed.

She was tired of letting things happen to her. It was time to fight back.

"EVERYTHING HAS BEEN quiet all night," Marcos Costa told Cole as soon as he drove up next to the car.

Cole's youngest brother may not have shared his blood—they'd met at a foster home as kids—but they'd formed a bond that went deeper than genetics. After Shaye had spent several hours in the forensics lab, Cole had driven her home and then promptly called his two brothers to see who was available to watch her house until he got off work. Their middle brother, Andre, was on a mission for the FBI, but Marcos had been free.

Now it was 3:00 a.m., and everything looked quiet on Shaye's street. Her house was situated on a corner lot in a cute little neighborhood that boasted its fair share of picket fences and young families. The kind of place where a stranger skulking about would be noticed.

Still, it was Shaye. He wasn't leaving anything to chance. And his youngest brother worked for the DEA, so he had plenty of experience spotting suspicious characters.

"Thanks," Cole said through his window as his car idled next to Marcos's.

"No problem. We all love Shaye." Marcos glanced past Cole at his partner, Luke, in the passenger seat and nodded hello. "Is there a reason we're doing this on the street instead of in her house?"

"She doesn't know you're here."

"Yeah, I got that," Marcos said with a dimpled smile. "I'm wondering why exactly."

"She refused police protection." Luke Hayes, Cole's partner on the force for the past three years, spoke up. "Officially we can't force her."

Marcos frowned. "But if someone's gunning for her—"

Cole didn't have to turn his head to feel Luke's glance as he replied. "No one is gunning for her. The shooting that happened earlier this evening looks random."

"Ah." Marcos nodded knowingly. "Got it."

"It's a precaution," Cole said, not bothering to

hide his annoyance at what Marcos and Luke were clearly thinking. That he was overreacting because it was Shaye. That no matter how far out of his league she was, he was still going to be there whenever she needed him.

"Don't worry," Marcos said, starting his engine. "I don't mind. But right now I'm going to head home and get a little sleep." He started to shift into Drive, then paused and asked, "Shouldn't you get some of that yourself?"

"That's why Luke is here."

Marcos grinned again. "You're going to nap while he keeps watch?" He peered at Luke and joked, "All that Marine training means you don't actually need sleep?"

Cole's partner had been in the Marines before becoming a police officer.

"Ha-ha," Cole said. "We're going to take turns getting a little shut-eye."

"Good luck," Marcos said. "Call me if you need anything, okay?"

"You got it." As Marcos pulled away, Cole eased into the spot his brother had chosen at the corner of the street. It was a perfect vantage point since it gave him a good angle on the two sides of Shaye's house that abutted streets. The remaining sides of her house were bordered by neighbors' yards, and they would be trickier for someone to approach.

Cole shut off his truck. It was a typical November night, hovering near forty degrees, but Cole didn't want the running engine to draw any attention from the neighbors, in case anyone was a night owl. Besides, he and Luke were used to working in uncomfortable conditions. Both of them had been patrol officers before being bumped up to detectives.

They sat in silence for a few minutes, checking the area, and then Luke asked, "Have we officially released her car yet?"

Shaye's car was still at Roy's Grocery, where the parking lot had been roped off so he and

Luke, along with a handful of cops working with them on the case, could pull evidence. They'd finished an hour ago, but Cole figured he'd tell Shaye in the morning.

"Technically, yeah. I thought I'd take her to pick it up tomorrow."

"Or just have it towed," Luke suggested. "She'll need that bullet hole repaired."

The gunman had fired three shots. One had hit the driver's door of Shaye's car, another had hit the back tire of the grocery store owner's car and the third had gone into Shaye. He'd asked the forensics lab to put a rush on reviewing the bullets, but they'd looked insulted he'd even asked. Shaye was one of them. They were already rushing it.

"We hear anything yet about those security cameras?" Cole asked. Although the camera at the grocery store wasn't real, there were others nearby they were checking. He'd probably have heard if there was news, because he'd made sure everyone working the case knew they should call him at any hour with updates. But he'd also spent several hours this evening at the hospital while Luke headed up the investigation. It was possible he'd missed something.

"Not yet," Luke replied, but he dutifully pulled out his phone and tapped in a text, then shook his head a minute later. "They haven't found the guy on any cameras yet."

Cole wasn't surprised. The grocery store wasn't in a highly commercial area, and it didn't get much criminal activity, either. There weren't as many security cameras as there would have been if the shooting had happened in another area of town. He wondered if that had been the shooter's intent.

"Shaye's got bad luck."

"What?" Cole shifted in his seat to face Luke, who always looked serious, with his buzz cut leftover from the military and his intense greenish-blue eyes.

"That's all this was. We went over her time-line. She was at work until eight, and then she drove straight to the grocery store, which she said she hadn't originally planned to do. If someone was after her specifically, that means they would have had to watch the forensics lab from at least five and then followed her. And in three hours, sitting outside a police station, don't you think someone would have spotted him?"

Cole nodded. He knew it was true. All the evidence said this had nothing to do with Shaye. Still, ever since he'd shown up at that shooting, his instincts had been buzzing the way they always did on a case when he knew something was off. And it was telling him there was more going on here.

"If it was random, meant to be a spree shooting, then why did he wait until the place was almost empty?"

Luke frowned. "Yeah, that bothers me, too. But he ran into the parking lot. Maybe he'd been coming from committing a crime and Shaye was in his way."

"We didn't have any reports that would match up," Cole reminded him.

"Not yet. Or maybe he planned to keep going—run though the grocery store lot, taking out anyone there, then move on to the rest of the businesses on the street. There are a couple of restaurants that were pretty full."

It was one of the reasons they didn't have any witnesses yet. It seemed counterintuitive—the shooter had run toward businesses full of people—but on a Friday night, it meant the music was loud, the patrons were drinking and no one heard a thing. Except for Roy still inside the grocery store, who'd sheltered in place and called the police.

"That's possible," Cole agreed, but he still couldn't shake the dread gripping him, saying Shaye had a direct connection. Because Luke was right about one thing: how unlucky could one woman be? Two attempts on her life in a year?

"Today is almost a year to the day of the shooting at the station," Cole said, even though he knew Luke didn't need the reminder. Luke had been there, too; he'd run out right behind Cole, firing back at the gang members, completely outgunned with their service pistols against semiautomatics.

"Yeah, and that's why I'm sitting in this car with you instead of in bed at home," Luke replied. "Because I think we got everyone in that gang. But they've all got families, too."

Cole nodded. It hadn't occurred to him that a gang member's family member might be trying to get revenge on Shaye for speaking up as a witness in the trial earlier in the year. His thoughts had always been on the families of the three officers who'd died that day. But his and Luke's bullets had killed two gang members at the scene, and four more had died in subsequent raids, because they'd pulled weapons instead of throwing up their hands when police came to arrest them. Any one of those men—or the ones who'd landed in prison—could have family or friends desperate for revenge.

"That theory has the same problem, though," Luke said. "If Shaye was a specific target, someone followed her to that grocery store. And if we're talking about someone affiliated with a gang, yes, they wouldn't be afraid to stake out a police station, but I doubt they'd be subtle enough to get away with it."

"True. And if we're looking at that kind of revenge, wouldn't someone want us to know it was them?" Cole added. "Or go after the station too? Both of us instead of just Shaye?

I don't like the timing, and it seems way too coincidental that she's targeted by gunmen twice—"

"She wasn't targeted before," Luke cut him off. "They had no idea she was involved in the digital analysis that got us the lead we needed on the gang leadership in the first place. They were there because we'd been investigating. She just happened to be on our side of the parking lot."

A fresh wave of guilt washed over Cole. He knew why she'd been by the station doors, when she should have been on the other side near the forensics lab, out of the line of fire. Most days they'd ended around the same time and stood outside chatting for ten or twenty minutes before going their separate ways. That day, he'd been late, caught up in paperwork. And she'd almost paid with her life.

"Well, still," Cole said, hoping Luke didn't

notice the new tension in his voice, "she's been shot at twice in just over a year. I don't like it."

"Me, either," Luke said, then swore.

"What?"

"Here she comes."

"What?" Cole said, spinning back toward the direction of Shaye's house.

His partner was right. Shaye was storming their way, her injured leg dragging a little behind, her hands crossed over her chest and a furious look on her face. None of that stopped him from noticing she was heading toward them in a nightgown that was way too short and way too thin for this kind of weather.

His mouth dried up as he got out of his truck, rushing over to her side and slipping his arm behind her shoulders in case she was still off balance from her injury. Behind him he heard Luke step out of the vehicle a little more slowly.

Shaye shrugged his arm off. "What are you doing?"

"Keeping an eye on things," Cole said. "Just until we catch the shooter."

She scowled but didn't look at all intimidating in her nightgown. It was just cotton, basically a big T-shirt, but on Shaye it somehow looked sexy. Especially with her hair spilling around her shoulders, loose and rumpled.

"I told the chief I didn't need protection." Her words lost some of their anger as he continued to stare at her, trying to keep his gaze on her face. As if she suddenly realized what she was wearing, she tugged the hem of her nightgown farther down her legs, her gaze darting to Luke and back again.

Then she spun around. Just when he thought she was going to demand he leave and call the chief about his unauthorized stakeout, she called over her shoulder, "This is unnecessary. But if you're going to insist on being here, you shouldn't sleep in the truck. Come on. You can stay with me."

A million images rushed through his brain, most of them involving that nightgown on the floor, and Cole knew he should refuse and climb back into the truck with his partner. Instead he followed Shaye inside.

Chapter Four

Shaye tried not to feel self-conscious as she strode quickly back to her house, but she'd never been more aware of the swing of her hips as she walked, of her long, awkward limbs. She pulled at the hem of her nightgown, willing her cheeks to cool as she held the door open for Cole without turning around.

Mixed in with her embarrassment was annoyance. The chief had offered her protection, even though she could tell he thought it was unnecessary. She'd had only a moment's hesitation before she refused. And yet here Cole was anyway, deciding what was best for her.

She tried to shove back her frustration. Cole was just doing what he always did, what seemed to come naturally to him: protecting everyone around him, whether they needed it or not.

"I'll be right back," she said over her shoulder as she headed to her bedroom. Pushing the door shut behind her, she changed quickly into a pair of loose sweatpants and a T-shirt, cringing every time she moved her leg. The painkillers were starting to wear off.

She paused a minute in front of the mirror, combing her hands through her messy hair. There wasn't much she could do about the deep circles under her eyes, not without makeup, and she wasn't going to dress up for Cole. Not when he'd shown up uninvited, determined to look after her whether she wanted his help or not. And not when the sound of his car on the quiet street had woken her from an almost sleep.

When she returned to her living room, she

found Luke settled on her couch, his legs stretched out in front of him and his hands tucked behind his head. Somehow he managed to look relaxed and totally alert at the same time. She nodded at him and continued looking around, until Luke pointed silently into her kitchen.

That was where she found Cole, checking the locks on her windows.

Shaye let out a heavy sigh. "I always leave those unlocked."

He spun toward her. "What?"

"The front door, too. I just let anyone in who asks."

He frowned, giving her the kind of stare she'd seen him use on hostile suspects. "That's not funny."

She planted her hands on her hips, subtly resting more of her weight on her left foot as her whole right leg started to throb. Apparently when the painkillers wore off, it wasn't a gradual thing. "I told the chief I was fine. *You* told me I had nothing to worry about, that this was an unlucky fluke. So why are you here? Were you lying to me?"

He leaned back slightly, and she could tell she'd caught him off guard. *Good.* She was tired of being scared all the time, tired of waiting for someone else to solve her problems. Tired of being in the dark about what was happening with cases that concerned her.

"No," he said slowly, looking her over as if he wondered what had happened to the nervous computer nerd he was used to.

She's gone, Shaye wanted to say, *and she's not coming back*. Except that wasn't the truth.

The truth was she *was* scared. But she needed to take charge of her life instead of letting things happen *to* her.

"Maybe you should sit down," Cole finally said.

Frustration built up in her chest, and she was

humiliated to feel tears prick the backs of her eyes. But she'd been shot today, so maybe she had an excuse. Her hip felt like it was on fire.

"I'm fine," she lied. "And I really don't need a couple of babysitters."

"If I'm a babysitter, my rate is ten dollars an hour," Luke called from the other room.

A smile quirked her lips, and she tried to hide it as Cole rolled his eyes.

"I wasn't lying to you," Cole said, taking a step closer, his hand hovering near her elbow, as though he expected to need to catch her if she suddenly fell. "There's no reason to suspect this guy was specifically targeting you. Because if that were the case, how would he even know where you were at that exact time? It makes more sense that he'd come here, beat the pathetic lock on your front door and do it in the middle of the night when you were sleeping."

She must have gone pale, because he was

quick to continue. "That's not what happened. You were at the wrong place at the wrong time—that's it."

"Then why are you here?"

"Because." His frown deepened, but instead of looking annoyed, he looked flustered.

She didn't think she'd ever seen him flustered. She tilted her head, curious. "Why?" she insisted. "If this was a total fluke and no one was targeting me, then what were you doing sitting on my street in the dark, watching my house?"

They were keeping something from her. She stared up into his light blue eyes, trying to find answers there. "It's gang related, isn't it? You think this guy wants revenge for last year?"

"Probably not."

"Then what?" she snapped, leaning even more on her uninjured leg. She wanted to sit, but he already had a height advantage. Plus, he was properly dressed in dark jeans and a button-down while she was dressed like a slob. And she needed answers. Needed the truth about what danger she was really facing. "What is it?"

"I can't take the chance," he barked right back at her.

She swayed, and it had nothing to do with her injury. "It *is* connected to the shooting from last year?" She had an instant flashback to being in that parking lot, bullets flying over her head as she hugged the pavement. To the panic, the absolute certainty she was going to die, and all the things she hadn't accomplished yet in her life.

"It's not connected to anything. Everyone thinks I'm crazy. But it's you, so..."

Her lips parted and she tried to find words, but there were none. Because all of a sudden, she saw what was underneath the anger and worry and frustration in his gaze. He was attracted to her. And not just in a he'd-seen-her-in-her-nightgown kind of way, but genuine interest.

The realization slammed through her, shocking and empowering. The pain in her leg faded into the background as she took a small step forward, then leaned in.

For several long seconds, he stood immobile. Then something shifted in his eyes, and all she could see was desire.

Shaye's heart took off at a gallop as his hands came up slowly and feathered across her cheeks. His thumbs stroked her face, and then his fingers plunged into her hair and his mouth crashed down on hers.

I'm kissing Cole Walker. The stupefied thought blared in her head as he nipped at her lips with his mouth and tongue and teeth until a sigh broke free and her lips parted. Then his tongue was in her mouth, slick against hers, sending shivers up and down her entire body.

She leaned into him, and thankfully he

dropped his hands from her hair to her waist, keeping her from falling. His big hands seemed to make a hot imprint through her T-shirt and for a second, she wished she'd worn something sexier. Then she couldn't think at all as he changed the angle of their kiss, and every nerve in her body came alive.

The scruff on his chin abraded her face, but it didn't stop her from pressing even harder, wanting more, wanting it now. Looping her hands around his neck, she pulled herself up on her tiptoes to eliminate any last space between them, and then yelped as pain shot down her leg.

Cole lifted his head, the fire that had been in his gaze doused with worry. "Did I hurt you?"

"No."

He held her at arm's length, still breathing hard. "I shouldn't have done that. I'm sorry."

Why not? she wanted to ask, but before she could get the words out, he'd reached past her and dragged a chair forward, pushing her into it.

"Did your wound open up?"

"No."

"Are you sure?" He reached for the band of her sweatpants, and she scooted sideways.

"Yes, I'm sure. I'm fine. Why—"

He stood up, backing away from her. "We came here to make sure you were safe. That was…that wasn't part of the plan."

Heat raced up her cheeks, this time from embarrassment. He kissed her like *that* and then told her it wasn't part of some plan? If it weren't for his use of the word *we*, reminding her that Luke was in the other room and had surely heard exactly what they were doing, she would have kissed him again.

Instead she nodded silently and got to her feet, holding up her hand when he tried to help her.

"We're friends," he said quietly. "I don't want to mess that up."

Shaye gave him a halfhearted smile, hoping the fact that she wanted to cry didn't show on her face. Because she could tell he was lying.

"Shaye—"

"Good night, Cole."

HE WAS AN IDIOT.

It was something Luke had been all too quick to tell him when he'd joined his partner in the living room after Shaye had headed to bed. As if he didn't already know.

He'd had Shaye Mallory in his arms, and he'd pushed her away. That was about as stupid as a person could get.

Except while everything about that kiss had felt right, he'd known it was all wrong, for a laundry list of reasons. He was here to protect her. She was injured. They were friends. But most of all, she wasn't the kind of woman you messed around with.

And there could never be anything long-term

between them because they came from different worlds. She was smart and educated, with the kind of earning potential he'd never have. She might have picked law enforcement for now, but Cole knew that if they weren't already, private-sector companies would be seeking her out soon, with huge salaries and perks. And she deserved that sort of life, one far from the bullets and crooks he dealt with on a daily basis. She deserved a man who was just as smart and educated as she was, someone who could give her things Cole never could. And he wouldn't pretend otherwise.

He cared about her too much to lead her on.

But was that exactly what he'd been doing for the past year? He'd known she had a crush on him when they met, and instead of staying away, he'd sought her out. He'd hover by the door each day before work, waiting for her arrive to start his day off right by chatting with her. He'd let her wait for him each day after work, let her beautiful smile and soft voice soothe away some of the crap of his shift.

He needed to take a step back, try to treat her like any other civilian who might need police protection. But no matter how many times he told himself that, he couldn't get that kiss out of his head. Hours later he could still taste the mint of her toothpaste, still feel the imprint of her lips on his. For someone who was normally shy and reserved, she'd been a firecracker in his arms. And he wanted more.

Luke had claimed the couch after Shaye had disappeared, leaving Cole with the big recliner in the corner. He'd slept in far worse, but as the sun seeped through the curtains, he realized he hadn't slept at all.

"Get over it, or do something about it."

Luke's voice startled him, and Cole glanced over, seeing his partner had one eye open. Luke's ability to sense movement even with his eyes closed was an asset in stakeouts, and the way he seemed to read people's minds was great for interrogations. But right now it was pissing Cole off.

"What am I supposed to do?"

When Luke raised an eyebrow, Cole snapped, "Don't be crude. This is Shaye we're talking about. I can't…"

"What?" Luke prompted. "Sleep with her? Date her? Tell her you've been obsessed with her since the day she walked through those station doors? Why not?"

Cole shot a glance down the hallway that led to Shaye's bedroom. Her door was closed, and he hoped she was still out cold. "We're friends. Let it go."

Luke shrugged. "I will if you will."

Grumbling under his breath, Cole gave up on sleep and trudged into Shaye's cheery red-and-blue kitchen. He dug around until he found the coffee, then started up a large pot. Before he'd made it back into the living room with his first cup, he heard Shaye come into the room and prayed she hadn't overheard his conversation.

But one look at her face, her chin up high, her cheeks tinged with red, her gaze daring him to bring up any of it, and he knew she had. A thousand curse words lodged in his throat, and he held them in, instead handing her the cup of coffee as a peace offering.

She cradled it between her palms and drank half the cup before she lowered it again, but he wasn't surprised. He'd heard her tossing and turning last night, probably the result of the painkillers not keeping up with the sting of her bullet wound. Or maybe the events of the night playing over and over again, all the possible outcomes racing through her mind the way they had in his. They were lucky she was alive.

"I'm going to get myself a cup of coffee—"

"And me," Luke interrupted, popping to his feet as though he'd slept ten hours.

"And then we're going to go through yesterday's timeline, make sure we're covering all of our bases," Cole finished.

Shaye nodded, but her hands shook around the coffee cup. "If this is going to turn into an interrogation, I need some breakfast first." She started to limp toward the kitchen, and Cole put a hand on her arm to stop her. She pulled it away fast, like his touch burned her.

Trying to pretend he hadn't noticed, Cole said, "I'll make breakfast. Just relax a little."

"There's nothing to make," she replied, pushing past him. "It's cereal and coffee. All my groceries are in Roy's parking lot. Unless you want frozen burritos for breakfast, that's what I've got."

He followed her into the kitchen more slowly, while Luke disappeared in the other direction, toward the bathroom.

She slowly set a few boxes of cereal on the counter, keeping her back turned to him, like she was waiting until her embarrassment fled. But when she finally turned, her cheeks were still flushed.

Shaye had never been good at hiding her emotions. After dealing with criminals day in and day out, he found it one of her most charming attributes, but he knew she hated it.

"About last night—"

"Don't." Her cheeks went from rose pink to fire-engine red.

"Shaye—"

"Just let it go."

Luke rejoined them at that moment, so Cole did. Instead of apologizing yet again—which probably wouldn't get him anywhere—he focused on her safety, and not the fact that he might have ruined their friendship. A ball of dread settled in his stomach, but he kept his mind on what he could do something about: eliminating the nagging feeling that this had been a hit.

"Let's go through your day yesterday, from the moment you woke up." Cole set down his spoon in cereal he'd barely touched. "Did you drive straight to work?"

"Yes."

"Your car was in the garage overnight, right? Did you step outside to get a paper, anything like that?"

"Yes, my car was in the garage, and, no, when I got in it to head to the lab it was the first time I'd left my house. And let me save you some time, because I've heard you talk to witnesses before. I didn't see anyone following me. Not yesterday, not in the past few weeks, not ever. And as far as I know, there's no one who has a reason to come after me, not with the Jannis Crew shut down."

"What about at work?" Luke asked. "Anything unusual there?"

Shaye frowned. "Like what?"

"Like anything. Coworkers acting strange

around you, someone who's shown an interest in you even though you've turned him down or made it clear you're not interested?"

Shaye shook her head slowly. "No. There's been a little turnover since I left a year ago, but most of my colleagues are the same. And the ones who are new all seem fine. It's business as usual at the lab."

Cole stared at her, wondering what that meant. He'd visited her in the lab a few times, and his presence had always surprised her. Not just because it was him and he didn't tend to come over to the lab, but because she'd been so focused on whatever digital device she'd been analyzing that she hadn't even noticed he was there until he'd told her.

Was she that oblivious all the time? Would she even realize if someone had been stalking her, waiting for the right moment to get her alone?

He wished he knew. But the truth was even

though they talked in the course of their jobs, and they had an unofficial agreement to meet up before and after work each day, he'd rarely seen her outside investigations. Even last month, when he'd asked for her help, it had been an off-the-books case. The realization momentarily surprised him, because she'd become such an important part of his life. And yet she was almost totally separate from it.

He wasn't sure if that said something about the strength of their friendship or just about his willingness to let people get close to him. Except he had plenty of friends, and to this day, he still tried to help kids coming out of the foster system because he knew how hard that transition was. So why? He wasn't sure, but he had a feeling if he probed that too deeply, he wouldn't like the answer.

"What about your job?" Cole asked when he realized the silence had dragged on a little too long. "What devices do you have right now?"

"I'm looking at computers from that corpo-rate espionage case. And the girl who's being stalked, to see if her computer was hacked. I've only been back for a week." She shrugged. "That's all I've got right now."

Neither were likely connections to today's shootings, but he gave Luke a meaningful look, and his partner nodded. They'd check both out. The corporate espionage involved two local competing businesses, and both sides had been repeatedly fined for violating vari-ous laws, but he doubted they'd resort to vio-lence. And the stalker was young; that kind of behavior always made him look twice, because it was often a gateway crime, but usually the ultimate target was the person being stalked, not someone connected to the investigation. Still, he planned to check every possibility.

"How about cases from last year?" Cole asked. "Anything you dealt with that's still in the courts?"

"Yeah, probably. I know there are a few that haven't gone to trial yet, but they're cases I worked peripherally. Nothing where I'm a witness. At least not yet. I guess I could still get subpoenaed."

Luke shook his head. "Probably not those. But let's make a list of all these cases—especially where you took the stand or your name would appear in the court documents—where someone went to jail."

Shaye glanced from him back to Cole. "Isn't this a waste of time? Shouldn't you be focused on witness statements or trying to track down this guy some other way?"

"We will," Cole assured her. "But no reason not to attack it from both directions."

She scooted her half-eaten bowl of cereal away from her and leaned on the counter. "But I'm not a direction at all, right? I'm just unlucky enough to have been shot at twice?"

Her words hung in the air. Cole wanted to

nod, like he'd done last night, and tell her this had nothing to do with her. But the more he thought about it, the more he worried that Shaye was at the center of something dangerous. And he had no idea what it was.

Chapter Five

"Let's go." Shaye unlocked the door to the lab and held the door for Cole and Luke, trying to calm her nerves. There had been hardly any cars outside the lab, but they didn't work weekends unless a big case required a rush analysis. But across the parking lot, cops' vehicles were lined up in what should have been a reminder of her safety.

She'd come so close this past week to feeling normal again. But maybe it wasn't ever going to happen now. Maybe her parents and her four brothers and sisters were right. She wasn't cut out for a job where bullets were involved.

Luke was gazing around curiously, but Cole stared back at her, like he could read her mind, and she ducked her head. If she wasn't cut out for a lab job, she definitely wasn't cut out for dating a detective. Not that a detective had asked her out. Just given her the best kiss of her life.

Pulling the door until it clicked shut behind her, she led the way through the sterile hallways. Past locked doors with the labels Biology/ DNA, Firearms/Toolmarks, Latent Prints and Toxicology. Down to the end, where a shiny new label marked "Digital Forensics," the most recent addition to the Jannis County Forensics Laboratory. Her territory.

Before she'd started—and last year when she'd taken the other job—digital devices had been sent off to the state lab. But it was one of the fastest-growing areas of forensics in Jannis, and Shaye was still surprised the job had been open a year later for her.

She used her key card to get into the room as Luke remarked, "Good security."

"Yeah, well, we take chain of command pretty seriously. And that includes making sure no one can access anything they shouldn't while it's in our possession. Everything gets logged. Even what I'm going to pull up for you will have a digital log that I accessed it, at what time and for how long." She'd helped set up some of those extra precautions last year as one of her first assignments on the job.

She glanced around her tiny space, jammed full of equipment—mostly computers. Her office was in the back with no windows, which often made her feel penned in, but today she appreciated it. And she was happy to have something to do besides sit around her house while Cole and Luke drove her crazy. They'd installed new locks on all her doors, exercised in her living room and called the station repeatedly for updates and to assign leads. And that had all been before 10:00 a.m. So when they'd wanted to go through suspects, she'd suggested they come here.

"Let's get started," Cole said, dragging her empty whiteboard to the center of the room.

He was wearing the same jeans and button-down from yesterday, just a little more rumpled. The short beard he always had was a tiny bit longer, too, and she fixated on it, remembering it scraping against her chin. She could almost feel his arms going around her again, the breadth of his chest pressed against her, big enough to make her feel surrounded by him. She shook off the memories, hoping her thoughts weren't broadcast across her face. But Cole was focused, his detective face on.

He jotted the words *Possible Suspects*, *Unlikely* and *Ruled Out*, then carefully underlined each one. "Any case you testified in or were involved in, now or last year. Pull them up, and let's get to work."

He sounded determined, almost enthusiastic,

and she supposed that was the kind of attitude you needed to be a detective, to slog through hours and hours of clues until you found the right answer.

She understood it because she could do the same with a digital device, dig and dig until it revealed all of its secrets. But hers was a totally different kind of quest, one fueled by years of shyness and feeling overlooked in her big, noisy family. Being the middle child in a family of seven meant you either had to demand attention or be content without it.

She loved her family. She *missed* her family, living so far away, when the rest of them had stayed in Michigan. But she'd needed to break out, make something of herself as *Shaye*, not just one of the Mallory siblings.

She settled into her well-worn chair. Time to see if the skill that had moved her past her sheltered, invisible life was threatening to destroy it, too.

"Let's start with the most obvious first," Luke suggested, snagging the only other chair in the room while Cole stood in the center of the small space, marker raised and ready.

"The Jannis Crew." Just saying the name made her feel a little ill. Shaye nodded and opened a file. Because she'd been in the line of fire, her boss had sent the digital devices they'd recovered after the shooting—computers, phones and tablets—to the state lab, so there'd be no conflict of interest. But she'd been on the stand, because she'd found the original trail to the leadership. And she was the only living witness able to identify the shooter.

The three officers who might have seen him had died on the scene. Cole and Luke had run out the station doors as the car was driving past. Forensics later discovered that their bullets had killed the two men in the backseat, but not the shooter. So Shaye had gotten on the stand, ignored her thundering heart and pointed directly at him, sending him to prison for the rest of his life.

"Well, we know it's not Ed Bukowski," Cole said, writing his name under "Ruled Out." "He was killed in prison last week."

Shaye jerked, spinning her chair to face him as an instant picture of the driver, one tattoo-covered hand draped over the wheel and the other aiming a gold-plated pistol out the window, formed in her head. "He was?"

"Crazy Ed found someone who wasn't impressed with his crazy," Luke said, using his gang name. "But put relatives on the *Suspect* list. The timing could fit. Maybe someone wants revenge for Ed's death. They can't go after the drug lord who shanked him, so they're going after the woman who fingered him, put him behind bars in the first place."

A violent shudder passed through her, and Shaye knew they'd both seen it. She spun to face her computer, sensing Luke and Cole sharing a look behind her back.

"Maybe we should do this part at the station," Cole said. "You provide us with the list, and we'll go through it."

"No. I want to help."

"There's no reason for you to relive—"

"I *said* I want to help." Shaye turned back, staring hard at Cole. "You don't need to protect me from this."

"That's my job, Shaye."

His job. Of course it was. It wasn't personal to him. But it was personal to her. "It's my job, too. So let's do this." She didn't give him more time to argue, just looked at her screen again and read off the next case.

Three hours later, the whiteboard was full. Most of the names were listed under "Unlikely" or "Ruled Out," but they had a handful of possible suspects that Cole and Luke were going to check out.

She stared at the list of names under "Possible Suspects," and the knot that had taken up residence in her rib cage eased for the first time since she'd walked out to Roy's parking lot. The only name that worried her was Crazy Ed, the man who'd been at the center of her nightmares over the past year. He may have been dead, but someone like that was bound to have attracted like-minded friends. Were there any left?

More important, were there any left who were willing to risk their own freedom for revenge? Because they couldn't have missed the massive cleanup Cole and his team had done after the station shooting. They'd have to expect any attempt to go after someone connected to that case would result in the same intense scrutiny.

Shaye let out a breath. "I don't think this had anything to do with me."

Cole and Luke looked from the board to her

and back again, and then Luke was nodding. "I agree. We're just being thorough."

When Cole was silent too long, Shaye asked, "Cole? What do you think?"

"Chances were always slim that this was a targeted attack," he replied, but there was an edge to his voice that told her he was holding something back.

"But…" she prompted.

"But nothing. Luke's right."

She frowned, but before she could argue, the door to her lab burst open, smacking the wall and almost hitting Luke on the way.

He scowled at the petite woman with the pixie cut and wrinkled pantsuit who stood on the other side, and she fidgeted. "Sorry. Shaye, I'm glad you're here."

"What's up?" Shaye asked, hoping no one had noticed the way she'd jumped in her seat at the unexpected noise.

The woman in the doorway, Jenna Dresden, was one of the lab's best firearms experts, and one of Shaye's closest friends here. Or at least she had been, until Shaye had left last year. Since she'd returned, things had been a little strained. Maybe because Shaye hadn't stayed in touch over the past year.

"I looked at the bullets we recovered at the scene yesterday."

Cole and Luke gave Jenna their full attention. "What did you find?" Cole asked.

"Well, I can tell you the bullet was a nine millimeter. And I can tell you that it doesn't match up to anything shot from another gun we have on file."

Cole didn't have to say a word for Shaye to know exactly what that meant. Someone connected to Crazy Ed being involved just sank down to unlikely. Working other cases had taught her that gang members sold one another weapons, so they often ended up with guns that had been used in previous crimes.

"The gun's a virgin," Luke said. "So we

won't know anything until we match the bullet to the gun it came from."

At that point, Jenna could compare the striations from the bullets they'd retrieved from the scene with those in the weapon's chamber and see if they lined up. If they did, they had their weapon. And whoever it belonged to was probably their shooter.

"Afraid not," Jenna agreed. "I wish I had better news. And now I'm going home, because I've been here since last night."

"Thanks," Shaye called as the brunette headed back the way she'd come. She looked questioningly at Cole.

"Back to square one."

"So, someone connected to Crazy Ed is out," Luke said.

Cole frowned. "I guess so."

After Jenna had given them the news about the bullet, that was practically a foregone conclusion anyway, but Cole wasn't leaving anything to chance. So he'd bribed a couple of his fellow officers coming off duty with a pair of basketball tickets to go home with Shaye and watch her until he and Cole were finished.

After hours in the stifling heat of the station—the air conditioner was on the fritz—they'd tracked down anyone even remotely connected to Crazy Ed, which wasn't a lot. It made Cole sad for the little boy Crazy Ed had once been: parents both killed in a drive-by when he was ten. He'd gone to live with an aunt, who'd overdosed a few years later, and then he'd ended up in the system.

Unlike Cole, who'd managed to form a brotherly bond with Andre and Marcos inside what felt like his fifteenth foster home in eight years, Crazy Ed had found gangs. The rest of his gang was now dead or in prison, and if he had any family left, Luke and Cole couldn't find it. So no one left to avenge his death.

"He shot up a police station," Luke reminded him, clearly able to read the direction of Cole's thoughts. "He chose his path. Nothing we can do about it now."

"Yeah." Cole shook off his thoughts about whether Crazy Ed had ever really had a chance before he started dwelling on all the other kids he'd seen in homes over the years, kids he hadn't kept track of. Kids he hadn't taken on two jobs to provide them with a real home and ease their transition out of the system, like he had for Andre and Marcos. Because it sure hadn't been easy for him, suddenly totally on his own, not even a roof over his head when he hit eighteen.

The truth was, Marcos and Andre had saved *him*. By then they'd been his brothers, and Cole hadn't been about to lose the only family he'd ever had. So, he'd walked out the door of that final foster home on the day he'd turned eighteen, determined to do whatever it took to build a home for the three of them. It had kept him out of gangs, out of any kind of criminal enterprises. It had led him straight to the police force, somewhere he could make a difference.

"Shaye's current cases are also out," Luke said, crossing off those names on the whiteboard they'd brought from Shaye's lab and bringing Cole's attention back where it needed to be. "The business owners both have alibis. And so does stalker boy."

"And I haven't been able to find anyone else connected to the Jannis Crew with the means or opportunity to pull something like this off," Cole said. Every name on the "Possible Suspects" list had a line through it, so he stared at the few names left on the "Unlikely" list. "What about Ken Tobek?"

"Ah, the engineer. Well, he did his bit and got out. He's alibied, too—he was drinking beer with a friend from work around the time of the shooting. The guy says Tobek was at his house until past midnight. And that jerk got lucky anyway. I'd hope he learned his lesson."

He and Luke had taken the call a year ago from Tobek's wife, Becca, who'd claimed her husband was plotting to kill her. She'd had some suspicious bruises and they'd found a judge with a particular hatred for domestic abuse and gotten lucky with a warrant. They'd been about to give up on finding anything when Tobek's computer had gone to Shaye for one last try. She'd dug up searches on murder and body disposal he thought he'd deleted. When they'd gone to execute another warrant, they'd found him in the process of trying to kill Becca.

In court, he'd been cleared of attempted murder and found guilty of only assault. Tobek had spent thirty days in jail and as far as Cole knew, he'd kept far away from his now ex-wife ever since.

Cole crossed him off and moved to the final

name on the Possible list. "Derek Winters?" He'd been paroled for good behavior just last week, and his original prison sentence had been reduced for time already served by the time the case had finally made it through trial. Initially they'd thought he was going to go free, but Shaye had pulled apart the GPS in his car and proved his location during the kidnapping of a young girl for ransom.

Cole and Luke had been on the team to bring that girl home three years ago, and when he'd handed her back to her parents, he'd promised them they'd find the person who'd taken her. It had taken eight long months, but they'd finally arrested him, only to have some of the evidence deemed inadmissible before they even hit trial. Then Shaye had started at the lab, their first local digital expert, and the computer had been handed off to her for one last-ditch effort. Shaye's find had been exactly what they'd needed. It was actually less damning than what they'd originally had on him that they couldn't take to court because of a technicality, but it had put him away.

Cole would love to see him go back. "He's the right size and he's definitely bold enough to try something like this."

Luke shook his head. "Shaye said the shooter was white. Winters is light-skinned, but you think she'd mistake him for white in the dark? I don't know."

"Shaye wasn't the one who described the shooter," Cole said. "That was me. But I saw a blur of movement—a hoodie and jeans. Definitely a guy, but skin color? I basically saw his neck. My impression was white, but I could be wrong. Let's just check him out."

"Okay," Luke said, lifting his phone.

"What are you doing?"

"Starting with his parole officer."

Ten minutes later, Luke was shaking his head

again. "His parole officer actually *saw* him that night."

"That late?"

"Apparently, Winters is paranoid. Calls and asks for meetings all the time, wants to talk about the FBI agents following him."

Cole's eyebrows lifted. "Is the FBI looking at him for something?"

"Nope. Guy's jumping at shadows. His parole officer is ready to pass him off to someone else. But he's alibied." Luke stood and took the marker from Cole, crossing the final name off their list.

"I was so sure this was about Shaye…" Cole muttered.

"You ready to tackle this the right way?" Luke asked.

Cole scowled at his partner, and anxiety took up residence in his chest at the idea that he was screwing up the case.

"Look, we're doing this investigation a disservice by assuming Shaye was the target," Luke insisted, looking convincing with his ramrod posture drilled into him by the military and the intensity on his face. "We're letting valuable time pass when we need to be approaching this like any other case, without presumptions. Start with what we know for sure and look at all the possible avenues."

Cole knew guilt was going to keep him up tonight as he nodded. His partner was right. He'd been so blinded by fear for Shaye that he'd let it impact the case, something he'd never done in all his years as a police officer. It was time to start thinking like the professional detective he was.

"Jeez," Luke said. "Nobody died. Wipe that despair off your face. She's one of us. We had to be sure. But let's start over and find this guy. Make him pay, whether Shaye was his intended target or just the result, okay?"

"I'm on board with that," Cole agreed just as his cell phone rang.

He would have ignored it, except it was one of the officers watching Shaye. Putting the call on speaker, he asked, "Hiroshi, what's up?"

"We're coming back in." The intensity of Hiroshi's tone made even Luke freeze.

Cole grabbed his weapon instinctively. "Why? What's happening?"

"We've got a tail. Rusted-out old Taurus, used to be blue, a real junker. He picked us up after we stopped at the store to get Shaye some groceries, and he's been with us ever since. We quit heading for her house and turned around, but I don't know how long until he realizes he's been made."

"Any way you can flank him and get a plate?" Luke asked.

There was a pause; then Hiroshi replied tightly, "I'm in Maryland traffic. This isn't a military op, man." He read off his location and direction. "See if you can go the other way and get behind him. Meantime, in case this is a shooter, I'm not taking chances. We're coming in."

"We're on our way," Cole said, putting himself on Mute but keeping Hiroshi on the line as he looked at Luke.

His partner grabbed his keys and swore like the Marine he'd once been as they raced for the front of the station. "I was wrong."

Cole glanced at him, eyebrow raised.

Someone *is* after Shaye."

Chapter Six

"Stay down," the officer in the front passenger seat—Hiroshi something—told her.

Shaye crouched even lower in the backseat of the police vehicle, behind the cage like a criminal. Panic danced in her chest as the car slowed to a near stop. The doors didn't open from the inside. She was trapped in this tiny space, just her and the groceries she'd grabbed from Roy's, determined to return there to prove to herself she could do it.

What had she been thinking? Had he been staking the place out, waiting for her?

A sob caught in her throat, and she swallowed it down. Who wanted her dead? And why?

The car started moving again, and then Hiroshi's partner, Wes, swore, speaking into his partner's cell phone. "He realized we made him. He just turned off, hopped the curb and headed for the freeway."

"He must have figured out where we were leading him," Hiroshi said softly.

Shaye was relieved. She knew she should have hoped he kept following, gave the police a chance to pull him over or even just find a way to get a license plate number. But she also knew that bullets weren't going to be flying again, and right now that was what mattered.

"What's the plan?" Wes asked.

"Bring her in," Cole's voice came over the speaker, calming Shaye's nerves. "I'm going to talk to the chief, see if we can get a helicopter up, try to spot the car from the air."

"Unlikely," Wes replied. "From that freeway, he can get onto—"

"Yeah, I know," Cole cut him off. "Just bring Shaye in."

"On our way," Wes replied tightly and hung up.

He started to say something else, but Hiroshi interrupted him. "Relax. You know what this is about."

What's it about? Shaye wanted to ask, but she was suddenly too exhausted to follow the conversation. Instead she asked, "Can I get up now?"

"Stay down," Hiroshi replied, shooting her an apologetic smile. "Just in case."

So she did, feeling foolish instead of terrified now as she kept her face pressed close to the vinyl seats, easy for wiping down after suspects left blood or puke or whatever else in here. She could practically smell the forensic material all over the backseat now that she wasn't busy bracing herself for the sound of gunshots.

Hiroshi and Wes were sitting straight, only the metal of the cage protecting them, even as they'd taken precautions for her safety. Hiroshi had recently married, and she'd seen the pictures Wes kept tucked inside his hat, two curly-headed boys that looked just like him.

Here they were, putting themselves on the line for her, and she couldn't even give them something to go on. Except for the cases she'd worked that Cole and Luke were running down now, she didn't really have enemies. Did she?

Who hated her enough to try to kill her twice in two days?

Sooner than she'd expected, the door was wrenched open and Cole was reaching inside, unhooking her belt and helping her out. Her feet were embarrassingly unsteady as he and Luke rushed her into the station.

"My groceries are still—"

"We'll get them," Luke cut her off.

"Thank you," she called behind her to Hiroshi and Wes as Cole and Luke continued to help her past the secure doorway and into the inner sanctum of the station, until she was in the center of the bullpen. She found herself settled in a surprisingly comfortable chair at Cole's desk, and then the two of them were off again, warning her to stay put.

The bullpen was quieter than she would have expected, even on a weekend. A pair of officers stood at the other end of the room, drinking coffee and talking quietly, but the rest of the room was empty. She'd been in the station before, but she suddenly realized she'd never been back here, where Cole worked every day.

Curious, she glanced around, taking in the bulletin board on one wall, a watercooler beside it. The door to a tiny break room was next to that, and the bullpen itself was filled with desks, broken up into little groupings. It actually looked like a lot of offices, until you got down to the little details. The Wanted posters on the bulletin board and the case timeline on another wall. The handcuffs tossed over a stack of case files on one desk, the gruesome crime scene photos tacked up on a half-built cubicle wall, the labels by type of crime on the huge file cabinet behind Cole's desk.

Cole's space was organized, which was no surprise. *He* was organized, always on top of everything. It was all job focused, a computer on one side and a notepad in the center, all his case files locked up like they should be. On the other end of his desk was a photo, and Shaye couldn't help herself. She picked it up.

It was obviously him and his brothers as kids. Cole had the same reddish-blond hair, the same intense gaze. On either side of him, she recognized Andre's darker skin and the cleft in his chin, and Marcos's almost-black hair and dimples. Cole must have been about fifteen, which would have made Andre fourteen and Marcos twelve. Now, nineteen years later, the men were all in law enforcement, and they looked it, with muscles earned taking down suspects in the police force, the FBI and the DEA. Back then they'd been scrawny, three lonely boys who'd found a family together.

She didn't know a lot about Cole's history, except that he'd met Andre and Marcos when he'd moved into one of his many foster homes. They'd bonded instantly, and in the few times she'd met his brothers, she knew it was a bond that would never break.

She thought of her own family back in Michigan. They could be too rambunctious, and they could overlook her because she hid in the background, but they loved her. It didn't matter how far she traveled. If she asked, any of them would be by her side in an instant. It was something she'd taken for granted, part of her close-knit Midwestern heritage that had always been assumed.

What had it been like for Cole, alone at two years old, tossed from one family to the next until he made his own?

She didn't know how long she sat there, imagining Cole as a baby, then as a little boy, never knowing that sense of security and love she never really thought twice about. But suddenly Cole and Luke were back. Cole looked questioningly at her hands, making her realize she was still holding the picture.

"Sorry." She set it back on the desk.

"That's fine. It's me and Marcos and Andre."

She nodded. "I know. From when you met?"

"No, right before they sent us all to different foster homes."

She jerked in her seat, surprised. She'd thought they'd stayed together once they'd met—she never realized they'd been separated. There was so much she didn't know about him.

She'd been half in love with him for two years, and all of a sudden she wasn't sure she knew him at all.

He was staring at her quizzically, and she tried to wipe whatever emotions were showing off her face. "What did you find out? Do we have any idea who was in that car? Is it possible it was a fluke? Maybe he wasn't really following us?" she asked hopefully, even though she knew the answer before Cole spoke.

"No, Hiroshi said he saw the vehicle at the back of the grocery's parking lot. He thought it was empty, but the driver could have just been slouched below the windshield, waiting for you to come out."

"Why would he risk following me in a police car?"

"Best guess is he hoped they'd drop you off and leave," Luke replied.

"Which would suggest he doesn't know where you live," Cole added.

"So, what? Could this be random, like he picked me out at the grocery store, and that's the only place he knows to look for me?" The idea of being the focus of some psychopath was even more unsettling than someone coming after her because of a case.

"Those guys tend to stalk their victims first," Luke said. "It'd be a little weird if it was a wacko who just didn't know where you live. It's possible, but given the fact that he's managed to pick up your trail twice and get away from us, I doubt it."

"More likely someone followed you from the station, and that's the only place he knows to look for you besides work," Cole said, but he didn't sound totally convinced. "It makes sense if the reason he knows you is connected to your job."

"Okay, then it's probably about one of my cases, right? What did you discover about the suspects?" Shaye asked, trying to focus on the fact that she had the city's best detectives on the case and not that someone was tracking her again this soon after being run off by the police.

Luke shook his head. "Nothing promising."

"We need to start thinking about who else has a reason to hurt you. We'll start with connections you've made at the lab, outside of your cases," Cole added. "And until we figure it out, I don't care if this guy only seems to know about your lab and the store. You're not going home. You can stay with me."

"WHAT MADE YOU become a detective?"

"What?" Cole paused in fitting her groceries into his surprisingly full refrigerator and stared back at her. "I don't know. I wanted to help people, I guess. Plus the pay was decent, and I didn't need an advanced degree to join the force."

Was it her imagination or did he look embarrassed when he talked about not having gone to college? She thought about telling him that he was one of the smartest people she knew, but she figured that would make him more uncomfortable. Instead she asked, "How long have you lived here?"

She glanced around the galley kitchen. It was small but clean, with dark-wood cabinets and pots and pans hanging overhead that clearly saw regular use. She tried to imagine Cole cooking, and she liked the picture she conjured up. Especially when she imagined herself in the kitchen helping him. She pushed the image away. It was too domestic. It didn't matter how much she'd been drawn to this man since the moment she'd met him—they had a work relationship. And she knew he'd never cross that boundary—at least not more than the kiss they'd shared in her kitchen.

"Couple of years," Cole said, not reading the direction of her thoughts for a change. "Thank goodness my brothers are smart. They both got scholarships, so that cut down on the debt. But it was tiny apartments for years."

Shaye took a minute to digest that. "You supported them? Like a parent?"

She hadn't had even a part-time job during college. She'd gotten a small scholarship, too, which had helped, because her parents had five kids to put through school. But they'd been adamant that she focus on school and not worry about working until she was finished. They'd even let her move back home after graduate school while she applied to jobs, until she was on her feet and had a little nest egg.

She'd had it so easy compared to Cole. At every turn, he'd chosen the more difficult route simply to help others. He was doing it still, with his job.

The more she learned about Cole, the more obvious it became how different they were, how far out of her league he was. But it didn't stop her from wanting to know even more.

He shut the fridge and picked up the overnight bag he'd carried in for her. "What's with the third degree? You looking to switch jobs, become a detective, too?"

"No." She leaned against the counter, blocking his way. "But you called us friends earlier, right?" Back when he'd said kissing her was a bad idea.

He nodded slowly, like he thought he was walking into some kind of trap, and she tried not to notice how good he smelled, standing this close to her. An intoxicating mix of spices and musk.

He'd taken off his button-down when they'd walked in, and the T-shirt he wore underneath stretched tight against his chest, outlining muscles her hands itched to touch again. She clenched them at her sides. "So why don't

I know this stuff about you already? I've never even been to your house."

"Neither have most of the guys at the station." He seemed to realize that was the wrong thing to say as soon as he blurted the words, because he backtracked. "It's not really set up for entertaining."

"Sure it is." She'd seen only the kitchen and the family room right off the entryway. It was cozy, the kind of place she could imagine tons of friends crammed in, eating Cole's barbecue and watching a game. It would probably be rowdy, sort of like a family gathering at her house. Cole might not have any blood relatives, but she wasn't the only one drawn to him. Everyone at the station respected him, treated him like a friend. She wondered why most of them had never been to his house.

He scooted past her, barely fitting between her and the counter, his body brushing hers in a way that had her replaying yesterday's kiss in her mind. From the flash of awareness in his eyes before he turned his head, so was he.

From the moment she'd met him, she'd put him up on a pedestal: her ideal, unattainable man. As a couple maybe they'd never make sense—she didn't know what kinds of women he dated, but she knew he wasn't shy. He went after what he wanted, and he'd never chased her. Not even close. But there was no question he was attracted to her.

She lived her life cautiously, always had. The biggest risk she'd ever taken was moving across the country for a job, but plenty of people did that without a second thought. Maybe for once she needed to stop thinking about all the consequences, stop worrying about the fact that there was no future for her with a man who ran into gunfire without hesitation. Maybe it was time to live for today.

Cole was heading into the family room, clearly expecting her to follow, probably planning to get back to work, tracking down anyone with a reason to hurt her.

The reminder strengthened her resolve. There was actually a gunman hunting for her. If he caught up to her, what would she regret not having done in her life?

Right now every answer she could think of involved Cole Walker.

She took a fortifying breath and followed him. It was time to stop having regrets.

Chapter Seven

Who was gunning for Shaye?

Luke wasn't wrong about serial criminals. Anyone savvy enough to have tracked Shaye twice in two days from a police station—if he'd spotted her in the regular course of her life—would have figured out where she lived by now. Except obviously this guy hadn't. Unless he was purposely trying to draw police attention. Cole frowned, liking that theory even less.

The police had stopped him. So far. Which meant he probably didn't know where she lived. Which told Cole that he'd first spotted

Shaye at the lab. And if he and Luke were right, it wasn't connected to one of her cases. Maybe a colleague? But anyone employed at the county lab had extensive background checks. Had someone slipped through, someone with a vendetta against hardworking, easygoing Shaye?

He spun around, expecting to find Shaye seated on his couch, ready to brainstorm. "We need to find…" He trailed off as he discovered she wasn't anywhere near his couch.

She was inches away from him, so close she'd actually had to back up when he'd turned to face her. And she was staring up at him with determination.

How had she gotten that close without him realizing? All his senses kicked into overdrive as a crisp ocean-breeze scent he always associated with Shaye floated around him. He doubted she wore perfume, so he guessed it was her soap or maybe her laundry detergent, something that shouldn't have been a turn-on but on her was. He noticed the cluster of freckles across her nose and cheeks, so faint she could have hidden them with makeup, but she didn't. He realized what a gorgeous shade of brown her eyes were, like a bottle of expensive scotch. Then her pupils dilated until he could hardly see golden brown at all, and her arms slid slowly over his chest to hook around his neck.

His skin tingled through his T-shirt from the light touch, and it should have been a warning to back away. He'd just promised himself he was going to treat her like any other victim. But then hurt flashed in her eyes as he didn't take what she was offering, and he ignored all his good intentions and gave in to temptation.

She was only a few inches shorter than him, so he didn't have to lean far to claim her lips with his. The second they touched, she let out a sigh and tunneled her hands in his hair. She tasted like cinnamon.

And this was a mistake, because the taste of her was addictive, rapidly eliminating all sane thoughts from his head as his hands slid over her slim hips and up underneath the back of her T-shirt. Her skin was ridiculously soft, her waist insanely tiny. His fingers crept around to the front, playing over her rib cage as her grip on his head tightened and the pace of her kisses grew frantic.

He backed her against the wall, needing less space between them, and his whole body thrummed at the feel of her, but even that wasn't enough. His hands slid down, ready to grip her butt and lift her, let her wrap those amazing legs around him so he could take her to his bedroom. Then sanity hit. He yanked his hands away just before he hurt her injured leg and pulled back.

She stared up at him, her chest rising and

falling too fast, her lips swollen and her eyes unfocused. She blinked, then took a step closer.

Cole held up a hand, trying to get control of his own breathing. If he didn't stop now, he was going to let her rock his world, and they'd probably both regret it later. Well, maybe he wouldn't, but she surely would when he told her they'd never be anything more than co-workers and friends.

Who was he kidding? he wondered as the desire in her eyes slowly turned to uncertainty. He'd never felt so out of control in his life. Every time he saw her, he lost all focus. And right now, this was about more than being distracted at his job. It was about her life.

The thought broke through his haze of need, and he backed away even more. "This isn't a good—"

"Don't say it," Shaye cut in. "Just…if things go wrong, I wanted to do that once more." She slipped sideways from the wall, away from him, then lifted her head, a completely different determination on her face now. "So I don't need a lecture about our friendship. I won't do it again. Let's catch this jerk so I can get on with my life."

She wouldn't do it again? That was exactly what he needed. But it only made him want to pull her toward him and change her mind.

He stepped back farther, trying to get his body in tune with his head. The sooner they solved this case, the sooner things could go back to normal. Except would he ever again be able to stand and chat idly with Shaye at the beginning and end of each workday, without imagining her body plastered to his? Without remembering the perfect fit of her lips, the softness of her hair through his fingers, the way her body melded to his like a puzzle piece?

He swore under his breath, and she gave him a perplexed look as she settled on his couch, straightening the shirt he'd twisted in his haste to feel her skin.

"That car was distinct."

"What?" He blew out a breath, trying to catch up.

"The car," she repeated, like he was slow. "It was a total piece of crap. It looked like it shouldn't have even been running. I only saw it for a second," she added quickly, "before Hiroshi made me duck. But there's got to be a way to track something like that, right? If he's a regular at the grocery store, maybe Roy knows who drives a car like that."

She was right. Tracking down suspects with a motive to hurt Shaye wasn't getting them anywhere. And even though the new incident pretty much guaranteed the shooting was no fluke, Luke was right, too. Cole needed to tackle this case like any other, by following the trail of evidence. Especially if they were wrong and they were dealing with a serial killer, maybe one who'd spotted her so recently he hadn't yet tracked her to her house. Someone like that wouldn't have any logical connection to Shaye—they often picked victims they didn't know. And a serial killer could definitely get so fixated on a particular target that nothing would deter him.

Cole's mind clicked back into detective mode, and he grabbed his phone. "I'm going to get officers to run that down right now."

He made a quick call, asking officers to talk to Roy again. He was probably driving them all crazy. He knew he was driving his chief crazy, especially after he'd fought so hard to have a helicopter go up after Hiroshi's car had been followed.

The chief had actually given in, but it hadn't done any good. He'd also announced that the police would officially offer Shaye protection, but Cole had shut that down for now. The better option was to hide her. And if this guy hadn't found Shaye's house yet, he definitely wouldn't have located Cole's. The fact was as much as Cole trusted his fellow officers, he knew no one had the same personal stake in her safety as he did. It would make it tougher to be out investigating, but as much as possible he wanted her in his line of sight.

"Okay, what now?" Shaye asked.

She was staring at him expectantly, but he was having a hard time focusing on the case with her cozied up on his couch, her feet tucked underneath her. It made his house look homey in a way it hadn't since his brothers had moved out years ago. Like she belonged there.

He cleared his throat and got his head in the game. "Did you get a look at the driver at all?"

Her lips scrunched. "No. Just the car, and then Hiroshi was yelling at me to put my head down."

Cole nodded, making a mental note to thank

Hiroshi again when he saw the officer. Hiroshi and Wes hadn't gotten a good look at the driver, either. Hiroshi said he'd been wearing a hoodie again, which wouldn't look unusual in the cold. It had probably been intended to hide his face in case anyone spotted the car.

"Traffic cams," Cole blurted, and before Shaye could ask about it, he was dialing the station again, asking them to pull traffic cameras from around the area where they'd been followed. It was hard to avoid being caught on camera these days. All they needed was one good angle...

"Yeah, we're already on it," one of the other detectives told him; then suddenly Luke was on the phone.

"I've got more news."

"What are you still doing at the station?" Cole asked, glancing at his watch. It was almost midnight, and Cole was barely still standing. His partner had been up just as long—and while Cole had been parked in a chair beside Shaye's hospital bed last night, Luke had been handling the crime scene.

"The Taurus that was following Shaye today was bugging me," Luke replied. "I kept thinking that Crazy Ed had a really old one."

Cole sighed and settled into the chair across from Shaye, who was staring at him questioningly. "I don't know. He had a lot of cars, but I think most of them were newer."

"Yeah, well, I looked it up. He did have a Taurus."

"Where's that car now? Didn't most of his cars go up for auction?"

"Not this one. It wasn't worth anything. This car went to a woman named Rosa Elliard. And guess where Rosa was almost nine months to the day after Crazy Ed was arrested?"

"Tell me."

"Hospital. Having a baby boy."

Cole let that news sink in. "Crazy Ed has a son."

"I think so."

"But what does that mean? You think she found herself a babysitter and is running around in Ed's old Taurus, hunting down people involved in the shooting? Because I may not be a hundred percent on skin color or age, but I'm pretty sure it was a man who was shooting in that parking lot."

"Maybe she's got family who doesn't like the fact that Ed Jr. will never meet his dad."

"All right," Cole agreed. "First thing tomorrow morning, let's pay Rosa Elliard a visit."

"No car." Cole spoke the obvious the next morning as he and Luke walked up the short drive to Rosa Elliard's front door. Her yard was overgrown with weeds, the carport was empty and the houses to either side of her were boarded up.

"Not a great place to raise a baby," Luke said.

"Yeah, but shouldn't she be mad at Ed instead of Shaye?"

Luke shrugged. "She *should*, sure. But when we're talking about things she should have done, not having a baby with a gang member is probably on the list, too."

Cole didn't know much about Rosa. Her name hadn't surfaced when they'd swept up everyone connected to Ed's gang a year ago. Which meant she'd been on the periphery of his life—or people were trying to keep her out of it, trying to protect her from the hurt the police was bringing down on everyone involved in the gang's activities.

The details he and Luke had pulled up at the station this morning before making the drive to this dilapidated area of Jannis County said Rosa had grown up with a single father who worked three jobs. He'd apparently done his best to keep Rosa and her younger brother and older sister out of gang life. Rosa's sister had gotten out, gotten a degree, and made a life for herself. Apparently the same wasn't true of her brother, who'd dropped off the radar a couple of years ago. Or Rosa, who'd fallen in with Crazy Ed.

Cole stared at the flaking paint on the beaten-up front door and wondered what had gone wrong.

"Get your head in the game," Luke said, rapping his knuckles on the door. A minute later, he rapped harder.

"Maybe she's out," Cole said just as the door was whipped open.

The woman standing in the doorway with a baby cradled in one arm glared at them. Despite the neglect outside, Rosa and Ed Jr. were well dressed, and Rosa's gaze was clear, no sign of drug use like they'd seen with a lot of Crazy Ed's gang.

"What do you want?"

"Ma'am, I'm Detective Cole Wal—"

"Yeah, I know who you are," Rosa snapped, even as she rocked slowly side to side for Ed Jr., who blinked sleepily at them.

Cole forced himself not to look at his partner. Their names had been in the papers connected to Crazy Ed's arrest and trial, but that was the only way she'd know them. So why hadn't she been on their radar before now?

"We want to talk to you about the Taurus that used to belong to Ed Bukowski."

"Why? You want that, too?" she huffed.

"You still own the car, ma'am?" Luke asked.

Rosa's eyes narrowed. "You see a car here?"

"Who has the car now?" Cole asked, knowing she was lying from the way her rocking suddenly increased.

Before she could answer, a man strode up behind her. Average height and build, light brown skin and angry brown eyes.

Wearing jeans and a hoodie, he matched their

gunman. Cole's hand shifted a little closer to his weapon.

"Why are you hassling my sister?"

The man's eyes were also clear, no sign of drug use, but a lot of fury there. And peeking out the top of the long-sleeved T-shirt he wore were the edges of a tattoo on his chest. *A gang tattoo?* Cole wondered.

"Dominic Elliard?" Luke asked.

"That's right." Dominic elbowed Rosa back, stepping in front of her and trying to fill the doorway without quite the bulk to be able to pull it off.

"We'd like to talk to you about Ed's old Taurus. How long have you been driving it?" Cole asked.

"Are you messing with me, man? The police department doesn't pay you enough? You took all of Ed's nice cars, and now you're back for the junk?"

"No, sir," Luke replied calmly. "We just want to know who's driving it."

"It's sitting in a junkyard," Dominic said. "Now leave my sister alone."

Before Cole could get out his next question, Dominic slammed the door in their faces.

"He's been driving it," Cole told his partner.

Luke nodded. "Yeah, but where's the car now?"

Chapter Eight

"Do you recognize this guy?"

Shaye stared intently at the picture Cole held up of a man in his midtwenties with dark, close-cropped hair and square, masculine features. He might have been good-looking if he weren't scowling. And if the fury in his gaze didn't send chills through her.

She shook her head and looked up at him. "Who is it?"

"His name is Dominic Elliard. He's got a connection to Ed Bukowski. We're pretty sure he drives an old Taurus, and he looks like our shooter."

Fear started to creep back in when she heard Crazy Ed's name. They were back to the gang connection? But no matter how hard she stared at Dominic's picture, she didn't recognize him. "He doesn't look familiar."

She was still at Cole's house, restless after a morning stuck here. Sure, he'd sent his brother Andre to stay with her while Cole ran leads. And she liked Andre. But she felt like a burden. Even worse, she felt helpless again.

She wanted to be doing something. Even if there *was* a gang connection and she had no training, no weapon. She knew Cole would do everything in his power to make sure she was safe, but she was tired of being rescued.

Shaye pushed herself off the couch and faced Cole as Luke stood near the door, silent, arms crossed over his chest. The two of them had arrived a few minutes ago after being gone all morning, and she'd felt the difference in their energy level immediately. They'd spoken quietly with Andre, and then he'd disappeared into the kitchen to make coffee.

Shaye stared at Cole and tried not to let the fear in. Two days after the shooting, her hip hurt a little less, and she felt like she could move again. Or maybe that was because she'd just taken more of her pain medication. "How is this guy connected to Ed? And what does he want with me?"

"Crazy Ed has a baby. He must have gotten this woman pregnant pretty much the day he went away for good." Cole tapped the picture. "This is the woman's brother. They both knew exactly who Luke and I were without us needing to tell them, and there was a lot of anger there. The thing is I'm not sure why they'd be so fixated on you as opposed to the police."

He frowned. Shaye could tell he was mulling it over, that the pieces weren't quite fitting together.

"Maybe she's step one," Luke spoke up. "Because she's an easier target."

Cole glanced back at him, nodding thoughtfully. "So let's redirect his attention toward us."

"I don't think—" Shaye started.

"Bring him to us," Luke agreed, a hint of a smile curling his lips. "I'm up for it. Let's get him to stop thinking about Shaye. Remind him who arrested his nephew's father."

"Wouldn't—"

"Get him to come after us," Cole said darkly. "And then get him behind bars."

"Hey," Shaye said, taking an aggressive step forward that got both detectives to look at her. It was instinctive for cops—move toward them, and their attention snapped to you, regardless of whether you were a threat or not.

They were talking about purposely pissing off the friend of a crazy gang member just to move the target off her. The idea of him chasing after Cole and Luke instead of her didn't make her feel any better. Despite knowing they were armed and capable of protecting themselves, it made her feel worse.

"I don't want you putting yourselves in danger for me. It might be faster, but doesn't it make more sense to run down the car? Trace it to the crime scene and then lean on this guy?"

"We'll be careful," Cole promised as Andre came back into the room, holding out two mugs of coffee to her and Luke.

Luke took his, but Shaye shook her head, remembering from the last time she'd met Andre how he made his coffee. Cole looked amused her refusal, and he grabbed the cup when Andre offered it to him next.

After Andre disappeared back into the kitchen for a mug for himself, Cole whispered, "Wimp."

"It tastes like motor oil," Luke muttered.

"I can hear both of you," Andre called from

the kitchen. But when he returned again, he was smiling, a crooked grin that lit up his deep brown eyes.

It was funny. Cole and his brothers looked nothing alike, but there was something about them that pegged them as family anyway. And it was more than just the easy camaraderie they shared, the good-natured ribbing.

Shaye was staring at Andre, trying to figure it out, when Cole nudged her with his elbow.

"You met his girlfriend, remember?"

Was Cole *jealous*? From the quick glance Andre and Luke shared, Shaye realized they thought so, too.

Cole took a small step back, redirecting his gaze to Andre. "How long are you available to hang here with Shaye? I think Luke and I should dig up some more information and then pay Dominic another visit."

Shaye put her hands on her hips. "Did you not hear me? If this guy is running around town with a gun, do you really want to put a target on yourselves? You hid me, but he knows where to find you whenever he wants. If he's anything like Bukowski, he's not afraid of firing a gun at a police station."

"We'll be ready for him," Cole promised, like her opinion didn't matter at all.

"And I don't get a say in this? This guy is after me."

"Yes, and we're trying to change that," Cole replied tightly, as though he was trying to be patient.

She turned to Luke. "If it was someone else being targeted by a shooter, is this how you'd handle it?"

He opened his mouth, but Cole spoke first. "Every case is different, Shaye. If Dominic is coming after you because of what happened to Ed, then logically he should have a vendetta against us, too. I want him to deal with that one first."

The scene from a year ago raced through her head: the smell of gunpowder in the air. The feel of someone else's blood under her hands as she dropped to the concrete. The sheer terror of knowing she was next.

The relief she'd felt when shots had fired from behind her—*toward* the shooters—had morphed quickly to an even greater terror when Cole had run past her, followed closely by Luke. She'd been positive she was going to die, and that feeling had seemed to go on forever as the officers around her had been hit and she'd been all alone. Cole and Luke's bullets had found their marks quickly, and her fear for their lives had been brief. But it had been even scarier than thinking it was her about to be shot.

She couldn't go through that again, knowing Cole was luring another gunman to him. "You use this plan and I'm going home."

"You can't go home. It's safer—"

She cut Cole off. "You can't force me to stay here. So you find another way to catch this guy or I'm leaving."

"SHAYE'S GOING TO be pissed at you," Luke warned.

"We tried to trace the car," Cole said. "It wasn't happening. Besides, even if we hadn't paid Elliard and his sister another visit, he was still mad from earlier. He might have switched his attention to us even if we hadn't gone back."

"Yeah, well, now we're definitely on his radar. Watch your six on your way home tonight. You don't want to get him fixated on you just to lead him right back to Shaye."

"I hear you," Cole agreed, even though they'd seen no sign of Dominic Elliard near the station this evening. The two of them had been back for hours, taking one last crack at finding the car. But Dominic had nothing in his name. Not an old Taurus, not a house, nothing. He hadn't for years, which told Cole he was into something. And the second tattoo he'd gotten a glimpse of on the man's arm when they'd gone back to his house that afternoon suggested it was a gang.

"He's not starting up the Jannis Crew again," Luke said.

Cole nodded. It looked like Dominic had fallen in with the Kings, another gang that had gained territory when he and Luke had shut down the Jannis Crew. It always seemed to work that way: knock down one criminal organization and another one was waiting in the wings to take its place. Sometimes the fight seemed endless; it was always the same battle, just new opponents. "But any gang connection tells us he's comfortable with violence."

"Yeah, well, let's just be careful he doesn't recruit other members to help him out. I'm with you on distracting him from Shaye, but I don't want to get him so mad he brings friends in on his personal revenge mission."

"I doubt it," Cole said. "If the Kings' leader knew Elliard was shooting at anyone without the group's say-so, it wouldn't bode well for him." The head of the Kings was notoriously paranoid and even more notoriously protective of his status. Any hint of a member running something on the side and that person ended up in the Jannis County morgue.

"True, but you never know with these guys. Anyway, I'm not afraid of whatever Dominic Elliard can bring down on us. I've been in worse firefights. But I don't want to lose another brother. You hear me?"

Luke was aiming what Cole thought of as his Marine stare at him. Cole nodded soberly. He definitely didn't want to put Luke in danger, and he didn't want Andre and Marcos to have to deal with another loss if Cole got careless. "Yeah, I hear you. Whoever this threat is, I want him behind bars fast. I think getting him to do something stupid where we can control the area is our best bet."

"Well, you'd better make sure Shaye doesn't figure out what we're doing. Because I believe her when she says she'll take off on her own," Luke warned. "She's desperate to keep you out of harm's way, too."

"I'm a cop." Cole frowned. "I'll never be out of harm's way." Maybe he needed to remind her of that—remind her exactly why she shouldn't be looking at him like he was potential boyfriend material.

Remembering the way it had felt when she'd kissed him, his body disagreed. But his mind knew it was the right move. When this was all over, he would still be a cop, and Shaye would still be a forensics specialist—one who'd been through trauma twice working with the police department. He wasn't about to drag her further into his world, expose her to more of it, by dating her. When whatever was happening between them now burned out, where would that leave them? He couldn't imagine his days without their morning chats, without her smile to close out his shift at the station.

What if that smile was waiting for him at home? The thought filled his mind and refused to leave.

"…too bad."

"What?" Cole shook off thoughts of Shaye climbing into his car at the end of the workday and coming home with him and tried to figure out what Luke had been saying.

"I said, I wish the chief would let us run surveillance on this guy. It's too bad we don't have something more solid, so we could pull in additional resources, because Elliard's got just enough anger to be behind this. But I still can't figure out why he's targeting Shaye instead of us. He didn't react as strongly to her name as he did to our presence."

"Maybe he's doing exactly what we hoped, focusing on us instead of Shaye," Cole contributed. Truthfully, he was surprised by that, too. But maybe Dominic was a better liar than he seemed.

"I hope so. But for now I'm heading home. Otherwise I'll crash here again, and I'd rather sleep through a sandstorm than in a holding cell."

"Be careful."

"You're sticking around?"

Cole nodded. Andre had promised he was available as long as he was needed, and Cole was bothered by that car. Years of talking to suspects had honed his internal lie detector and there was no question Elliard had been lying about it being in a junkyard. But if it wasn't at his sister's place and Dominic didn't own property, then where was it?

"See you in the morning."

Cole waved absently, pulling up Elliard's

record again, looking for any connection he'd missed—someone who might store a car for Elliard. Three hours later, he had no new leads. Elliard didn't seem to run outside Kings circles, and none of them would risk their leader's wrath.

Giving up for the evening, Cole yawned and dialed Andre as he headed out to the parking lot. When his brother picked up, Cole asked, "How's everything there?"

"Your girl isn't happy."

"Why not?" Cole asked, refraining from commenting on the obvious. Shaye wasn't his girl.

"She suspects what you're doing."

"What do you mean?"

"Don't play innocent with me," Andre replied. "I've known you too long. And it looks like Shaye knows you too well. She's sure you're trying to get a gang member to come after you. Is that really—"

The rest of his brother's words were cut off by automatic gunfire.

Cole hit the pavement, and the cell phone slid out of his hands as he went for the weapon holstered at his hip. His gaze darted around the parking lot, looking for the threat.

And there it was—someone in a hoodie running toward him holding something much bigger than a pistol.

Cole swore as he slid behind the cover of a parked patrol car, wishing he hadn't been the last one at the station. He yanked his Glock free of its holster, knowing it was a poor match for the weapon aimed at him.

But he was a trained police officer, and he was sure the man shooting was Dominic Elliard. Gang members tended to rely on firepower rather than accuracy, and Cole could use that to his advantage.

Heart pounding, Cole got to his knees beside the wheel, listening for the pounding of footsteps. He needed to pinpoint the shooter's location so he could aim fast.

Before he could do it, more gunshots rang out. Cole looked back at the door, wondering if he could make a run for it.

Dominic Elliard had brought friends.

Chapter Nine

"Give me a gun," Shaye demanded.

"What?" Andre looked over at her from where he was pacing in Cole's living room, a phone pressed to his ear and his free hand locked in a fist. "No."

"We need to go help him!"

"Shaye, this is going to be over before we get there. I called backup. They're on their way."

Tears pricked her eyes, and Shaye blinked them back. She knew Cole had been going ahead with his dangerous plan. She'd known it, and she'd fought him on it. But she should have actually followed through on her threat and walked out the door. It would have brought him back home. It would have pissed him off but kept him safe.

"This isn't your fault," Andre said softly.

His deep brown eyes were soft, filled with understanding, but underneath was his own fear. He and Cole were so close. If something happened to Cole, it *would* be her fault.

What would she do if he was hurt? If he was killed? The thought made her chest seem to cave in, made breathing difficult.

"Luke is driving back to the station right now," Andre said, his voice still calm, probably a result of constantly running into dangerous situations with the FBI. "They've got patrol cops close. And my brother is a fighter. Plus he's smart. I've seen him go up against tough odds before, and he's good at turning them in his favor."

"These are gang members," Shaye said, realizing she sounded hysterical but unable to calm down. The longer they went without news, the more it set in what Cole was up against, all alone.

She'd been sleeping—or at least trying to sleep—when Andre's panicked voice had woken her. She'd run into the living room to hear him demanding help at the police station. And then he'd said he'd heard multiple automatic weapons firing.

"Why haven't we heard anything?" Shaye demanded.

"Keeping us informed isn't their first priority," Andre replied, but his ear was still to the phone.

She didn't know who he had on the line until he said, "How close are you, Luke?"

"You should go," Shaye told Andre. She knew he had to be desperate to go help Cole, no matter what he was telling her. "I'll stay here. I won't leave, I promise."

"Can't do it," Andre said, barely looking at

her as he listened to whatever Luke told him. Then he closed his eyes and let out a long breath.

"What is it? What happened?" A million horrible scenarios ran through her head until she really couldn't breathe. Then she could barely hear over a high-pitched ringing in her ears.

But she heard Andre's voice as he asked, "Is he dead?"

And then she was falling. The floor came up to greet her, and she couldn't hear anything more.

How many of them were out there?

Cole's pulse ratcheted up way too high as he glanced at the exposed station doorway. No way he could make it and use his key card to dive inside without being shot.

He'd been so certain that Elliard wouldn't bring backup. It was a stupid mistake, underestimating him. It was a stupid mistake to rely on his gun and badge as if they made him invincible. And right after Luke had made Cole promise not to make anyone plan his funeral.

Bullets were still spraying, way too many of them. He'd fired a few shots, but was pretty sure they hadn't hit their marks. Someone—he thought it was Elliard—was screaming, but Cole couldn't make out the words. A bullet hit the tire beside Cole, and the patrol car shielding him dropped on the left side. The windshield shattered, too, and glass rained down around him.

He was trapped. And he didn't have much time before the gang members decided to run around the car and shoot him straight on. Cole glanced around again, trying to find any way to increase his chances of surviving until backup arrived.

There was no question Andre had called in help. He prayed his brother wasn't still on the line, that he wouldn't hear the shot that killed Cole when it happened.

Cole shook glass off himself, trying to watch both sides of the car. The car suddenly sank again, until the entire right side was higher than the left, and he realized a bullet must have hit the back tire, too. An idea formed—it wasn't much of an idea, but it was the best one he'd had so far.

Praying no one would choose that moment to round the front of the car, Cole peered underneath. Locating a pair of legs running his way, Cole aimed and fired. There was a scream, and the man dropped, his machine gun sliding out of his grasp and skidding away from him on the concrete.

Before the gang members could realize what he was up to and try to target him the same way, Cole lined up another pair of legs and took another shot. A second man hit the pavement, and then he heard the most glorious noise.

Sirens, a lot of them, and getting louder.

The direction of the gunfire shifted, and he heard footsteps pounding as the shooters tried to escape. A car started up, and then shotgun blasts joined the automatic gunfire.

Cole's backup had finally arrived.

The engine rumbled on what must have been the shooters' vehicle, and then another shotgun blast sounded, followed by a noise like an engine failing. "Hands up!" someone screamed. It sure sounded like Luke.

Then there were a lot more voices, all at once. "On the ground! Now! Get down!"

Carefully Cole peered around the side of the car to see a small group of Kings members dropping their guns and lying flat on the pavement. Two more lay moaning and bleeding where he'd shot them. And then, way off to the side, in a spot where he might have had an angle to shoot Cole, was another man, clutching his chest and drawing in the kind of loud, hacking breaths that said he'd been hit.

Cole ran toward him, not lowering his pistol, and kicked the MP5 out of reach. The man had one hand pressed hard against the bottom of his rib cage, and blood spread out over his dark hoodie. From the wheezing sounds he made with every breath, the bullet had collapsed his lung.

Reaching down, Cole pulled the hoodie away from his forehead. "Dominic Elliard."

"Help me," Elliard rasped.

"We're going to need an ambulance over here," Cole called.

"Already on its way," Luke yelled back. "You okay?"

"I'm not hit. But Dominic here is."

After he finished cuffing the two men Cole had shot, Luke hurried over to Cole's side.

"I guess our plan worked," Cole said weakly.

"Yeah, but we were wrong about Elliard bringing backup."

Cole frowned, glancing from Dominic to the other Kings members and then back again. "I don't think so."

"What do you mean?"

"I didn't shoot Elliard."

Luke looked over at the patrol car Cole had been hiding behind, which was covered in bullet holes, the entire left side pockmarked. He swept the two men with leg wounds lying halfway between the gang members' car and the patrol vehicle, then the two other men being cuffed at the far end of the parking lot. "If his own gang shot him, why'd they bring him here to do it? There's only one car."

"Unless Dominic parked somewhere else and walked."

"Or they were all in it together and someone turned on him. Or just hit him by accident—

they did have semiautomatics and the Kings aren't exactly known for their marksmanship."

"I need help," Elliard rasped at their feet as an ambulance swung into the lot and one of the officers waved the EMT toward them.

"It's coming," Luke replied. "So what was the plan, Dominic? You do this yourself, or did someone above you order this hit?"

Elliard's eyes widened, and Cole knew he'd just realized what Luke was implying. Regardless of whether the others had come with him or come to hunt him down, if the Kings' leader *hadn't* ordered Cole's death, then Elliard had just guaranteed his own.

"Maybe you'd better talk to us," Cole recommended, holding back his anger that this man had just tried to kill him. "So we can protect you."

"My sister," Elliard wheezed. "My nephew. Please, don't let anyone hurt them."

Cole nodded at Luke, who stepped away and

made a phone call, as the EMTs bent down to look at Elliard's wound.

"Tell me what happened here," Cole said, bending close. Realizing he still had his pistol in his hand, Cole tucked it into his holster. Adrenaline pumped through him, giving him energy now, but he knew he'd crash hard later.

Elliard's lips trembled, and Cole couldn't tell if it was anger or fear or pain—or maybe all three. "Rosa has nothing. Ed promised to take care of her and the baby. And then practically the day after he found out she was pregnant—the day after he swore he'd leave that life and take care of them—he went and got himself arrested. If that wasn't enough, then came the police, taking away every little thing he'd owned, every last dollar that should have been Rosa's."

"Sir, try to relax," the EMT said, shooting Cole an annoyed gaze. "Maybe you can do this another—"

"So you decided to make the same mistake as Ed, shoot up a police station and land yourself in jail so your sister has no one to help her," Cole spoke over the EMT.

"Maybe if you'd left us alone," Elliard snapped, then groaned, his eyes rolling back in his head as the EMT pressed down on his wound. "But you just kept coming, like having loved Ed made Rosa guilty, too."

"Sir," the EMT said, trying to nudge Cole out of the way as his partner lined up a backboard and they rolled Elliard onto it.

"How'd you convince your friends to do this with you? Or were they here for you, Dominic?"

Elliard's gaze latched on to Cole's, filled with pain and panic. He blinked a few times and then sucked in a deep breath before his eyes closed and didn't open again.

"Get him in the ambulance," the EMT said, and his partner loaded him on, then jumped in, too, doing compressions on Elliard's chest. The first EMT raced to the front and got behind the wheel. Then the ambulance raced off, sirens blaring.

"PURE LUCK I wasn't shot…automatic weapons…five of them…gang members."

Cole's voice filtered back to her, disjointed, sounding farther away than he really was. She'd heard him arrive home ten minutes ago. Or maybe it had been an hour. Shaye had lost all sense of time since Andre had carried her in here, put her in the center of Cole's big bed and told her to try to rest.

That felt like days ago, but when she glanced at the clock on Cole's bedside table, she saw that it had been only a few hours. A few hours since he'd come in and told her Cole was okay. He was alive.

Just thinking about those moments when she'd thought he might have died made Shaye's heart rate pick up. She breathed in Cole's scent, still sensitive to it even though she should have stopped noticing by now. But it was all around her, rising up from his pillow. His room looked like what she would have expected—masculine and understated.

She didn't know if Andre had put her here because he thought it would be comforting or because he hadn't been thinking about it at all, just been desperate to get back on the phone for news of his brother. She couldn't believe she'd fainted twice in the past few days, when until this week she'd never fainted in her life.

From the living room, Marcos's voice joined Andre's, angry and worried. Marcos had arrived a couple of hours ago, too, shortly after they'd gotten the news that Cole was okay. He and Andre had both checked on her repeatedly, until she'd finally told them she wanted to sleep.

Sleep hadn't come, but she'd needed the re-

prieve from their worry, from the constant reminder that Cole had almost died tonight. The
panicky feeling in her chest still hadn't left,
and she had a sudden insight to what it must be
like for the wives of police officers. Did they
feel this way every day when their husbands
were on the job, this nonstop fear? How did
anyone live this way?

"You've got to stop trying to handle everything yourself for everyone you love!" she
heard Marcos say, cutting into her thoughts.

Cole started to respond, but Andre interrupted him. "We're all in dangerous jobs, but
you're making yours more dangerous."

They must have been close to yelling, because where the words had barely filtered
through the walls before, now she was hearing them clearly. Shaye felt a little guilty and
wondered if they remembered she was back
here. Maybe she should go remind them. But
she wasn't sure she could look at Cole right

now without bursting into tears or racing into his arms. And she didn't think he'd appreciate either one.

"Just like the fire when we were kids," Andre said, his voice softer now.

Shaye frowned, sitting up in bed and straining to hear.

"I'm sorry," Cole said. "I didn't want to put you through that." His voice sounded choked up. "I'm never going to forget those minutes thinking Marcos wasn't going to make it out."

There was a long pause, and Shaye thought they were just speaking too softly for her to hear, until Andre's voice carried to her clearly: "And knowing that if you weren't holding me back, you'd have run right back in there for him."

A new kind of pain wound around Shaye's residual worry. She knew only bits and pieces about Cole's childhood, but she'd once heard him mention a fire that had destroyed the foster home where he'd lived. How old had he said he'd been? Fifteen? She'd had no idea they'd actually been *inside* the house when it happened.

She couldn't help it. She knew she shouldn't, knew that if she were thinking more clearly, she'd stay put until she had her emotions under control. But she shoved the covers off and climbed out of bed, a little unsteady on her feet.

Then she walked into the living room, right past Andre and Marcos, and threw herself into Cole's arms.

Chapter Ten

Cole hesitated a minute, and then his arms went around her, too, pulling her tight against him. If his head wasn't turned slightly away, she could have leaned up on her tiptoes and kissed him.

This close she could feel him take in a deep breath and knew tonight's firefight had scared him more than he was saying. She could have sworn he was breathing in the scent of her hair before he set her gently away from him.

"I'm okay, Shaye," he said softly.

She stared up into the perfect blue of his eyes, noticing the furrows between his eyebrows, the tension in his jaw. A million responses rushed to her lips—wanting to yell at him and kiss him and tell him everything was fine now—but she just nodded.

"Are you sure the threat is over?" Marcos asked. Cole's youngest brother looked more serious than Shaye had ever seen him, no sign of his ever-present grin.

"Positive. Dominic is still in critical condition, but Luke and I interviewed the other gang members. We're still not sure if they were with Dominic or against him—they're not saying much—but one thing is totally clear. This hit wasn't ordered. At least not on me."

"Not like they're going to admit that," Andre said, sounding skeptical.

"No, but the head of the Kings just isn't that stupid. He actually called the station, making all kinds of noise about being a concerned citizen, but it was clear he wanted me to know he had nothing to do with it. And I don't think he was just backtracking. None of these guys are asking for lawyers, and it's because they want to stay in the cell. Whether they were helping Dominic or trying to kill him, they don't want to deal with their boss's wrath for disobeying his orders—or failing them."

Marcos and Andre were nodding as Shaye studied all of them. "So, you're saying you're safe?"

"I'm saying *you're* safe," Cole replied. "Dominic was dressed practically the same way as the last shooting. Even if he pulls through, he's going away for a long time."

"So I can go home?" Shaye asked, even though it was the last thing she wanted to do right now. She knew Cole hadn't been hit; she could see with her own eyes that he was fine. But she also knew it wouldn't truly sink in for a while, and she'd feel better if he was near her.

"No." Cole's tone was firm. "You're sticking close until we confirm whether these guys were with Dominic or against him. My bet is against, but I want to be certain. And I want to make sure he doesn't have anyone else who'd help him with this vendetta. Because Luke sent a patrol car to pick up his sister and her son to keep them safe, and they were gone. No sign of a struggle."

"A gang would kill them there," Andre agreed.

"We think Dominic probably took the Taurus—which we're searching for now—so someone must have picked her up. Most likely for the same reason we were there, but I'm not taking chances."

At his words, Marcos and Andre gave him identical raised eyebrows—which Shaye interpreted to mean "except with your own life."

Cole held up his hands, suddenly looking beyond exhausted. "I promise I'm going to be more careful."

They didn't look appeased, but Andre said,

"You're crashing. We'll get out of your way." He looked at Shaye. "Take care of him, will you?"

"I will," she replied, ignoring Cole's protest, and hoping his brothers hadn't told him about those embarrassing moments a few hours ago when she'd woken up to find Andre checking her head for signs of injury.

Then his brothers were gone, and it was just her and Cole, staring at each other. Energy sizzled between them, an awareness mixed with too many other emotions to untangle. On her side, anger and frustration and fear. She wasn't sure exactly what he was feeling besides the need to sleep.

"You should go to bed," she told him, and for one drawn-out minute, she thought he was going to suggest she come with him.

He said, "I can't sleep right now. I need to decompress a little. I'm going to wash the crime scene off me." He said it like it was any other case he'd been called to, instead of one where he'd been the intended victim.

Then he disappeared into his bedroom, leaving Shaye alone in his living room. She stood awkwardly, knowing the worry from tonight meant she should be crashing now, too. But she felt edgy, wired and anxious, and she wasn't sure why.

Was it really over this time? Was she truly safe? Or would she go another year and find herself in someone else's crosshairs, some other person in Crazy Ed's life they'd never known about?

Somehow, it didn't feel like it was over. Maybe because Cole had almost died a few hours ago, or maybe because Dominic Elliard was in the hospital and they didn't have the full story yet. But what if it never ended?

She'd worried from the start that things would never go back to the way they'd been when she'd begun her job two years ago. Now she was sure of it. She was never again going to have that naive certainty that she'd just be unraveling puzzles in a lab. She'd never again be able to have that pure, simple joy without a little fear mixed in. She'd fought so hard for this life, but did she want it like this?

She honestly wasn't sure.

"Shaye?"

Cole's voice was soft. When she spun around, she found him standing close to her, his hair wet from a shower, wearing different clothes. How long had she been standing here?

He brushed a lock of hair out of her face. "I promise you I'm fine. It wasn't as bad as it sounded."

"You're lying." His face was so close to hers, the scruff on his chin heavier than it had been this morning, the shadows under his eyes deeper. And the look in his eyes… She lifted her hand, unable to stop herself, and slid it over his cheek.

He leaned into her palm. "I don't want you to worry."

"I can take it." Could she? She wasn't sure, but not knowing all the details of the shootout meant she was imagining every possible scenario. Maybe the truth would be even worse than she could imagine, but at least if he was honest with her, she could help him deal with it.

He stared at her for another long minute, then slowly turned his face into her palm and kissed her, and the light touch seemed to dance up her arm. Then his mouth was moving over her wrist, making her pulse jump and her heart race, and up to her elbow. His hand followed, and he tugged her toward him.

An instant before his lips would have met hers, she stumbled backward, pulling out of his arms. "Cole—"

"I'm sorry. You're right." He shoved his hands in his pockets. "I said we were just going to be friends. I'm trying to mean it."

The look he was giving her was anything but platonic. She tore her eyes away from his before she caved and tried not to sound breathy as she replied. "I don't want to be a distraction."

"You're not a distraction." He sounded insulted.

"What I mean is, I want to talk about this. I want to know what happened." And she wanted to know why his brothers—the people who knew him best in the world—thought he was putting himself in danger. She didn't say it out loud, but he seemed to hear her thoughts, because he frowned at her.

"Andre and Marcos are overreacting."

"Okay, then tell me about the fire."

"The fire?" He was scowling now, but it wasn't really aimed at her.

"You said you wanted to be my friend—"

"We are friends."

"Then *talk* to me. Tell me the truth about something, about what happened tonight, about your life."

"You think I'm lying to you?" He yanked his hands out of his pockets, crossing them over his chest. "Honestly, Shaye, I spent the evening being shot at by gangsters with semiautomatic weapons to protect you! And you're accusing me of what exactly? Not being a good friend?"

"That's not what I'm saying." Wow, she was tired. It hit suddenly, draining her of all energy and making her doubt herself. Was she being unreasonable, pushing him because *she* was scared? Or was she right, knowing that to even begin to figure out how she felt about him, he had to really let her in?

It was probably a little bit of both, and right now, with emotions high, wasn't the best time to get into it. But frustration built in her chest, edging out the fear and confusion. "I just want you to trust me enough to treat me like your equal, instead of someone you have to constantly protect."

Her words came out defeated, and hung there between them until he shook his head and left the room.

"I WOKE UP and the house was on fire."

"What?" Shaye rolled over, looking groggy and way too tempting lying in the middle of his guest bed in another one of her oversize T-shirts.

"Back when I was fifteen," Cole clarified, sitting on the edge of the bed and trying not to let his gaze wander down to her bare legs. He should have waited until she'd woken up this morning, but he'd been up half the night thinking about how he'd ended their conversation.

This morning, after a few hours' rest and a little distance from the shooting, he felt bad about walking out on her. He still thought she was being unfair, but maybe if he laid it all out for her, she'd finally get it. They were way too different.

Her life was like one of those old-school sit-coms, with parents who were still married and a bunch of close-knit siblings. A comfortable life, a good degree and the chance to do the same thing when she married. That sort of world was so foreign to him, he didn't know where to begin.

He didn't really want to get into his past, or push her away, but maybe that was what he needed to do so both of them could move forward.

Tugging the sheet up her chest, Shaye scooted into a sitting position, suddenly looking wide-awake. Her hair was a mess, falling over her shoulders, rumpled on top of her head.

He'd never wanted to run his fingers through anything so badly.

"What happened?" Shaye asked softly.

Cole shrugged, his breath suddenly shallow like he was back in that smoke-filled hallway, desperate to get to his brothers before the ceiling caved in. "They ruled it an accident." But recently he and his brothers had had their doubts.

Shaye's fingers curled around his, and the light contact made his chest tighten.

From the moment he'd met them, Andre and Marcos had been there for him, but he was the oldest. He'd never had a real family before them, but he'd done his best to do the things a big brother should, which meant taking care of them as best he could. It was hard for him to lean on anyone else, maybe because he'd been tossed into foster care at two and never stayed in one place more than five years. It was a bad idea to rely on anyone, because you never knew when they'd be pulled away from you. His brothers had been different. Maybe Shaye was, too. Maybe she was right about him not trusting her.

"What are you thinking?" she whispered.

He squeezed her hand tighter. "I was taken

away from my birth family when I was two because of neglect."

She jerked, like the change in topic had thrown her, but then scooted even closer, and man if she didn't somehow smell like the ocean again. Maybe it was her shampoo.

As a kid he'd never seen the ocean, despite living relatively close to it all his life. As an adult, it had represented freedom to him: the ability to do what he wanted without foster parents restricting him or social workers evaluating him. Shaye represented freedom to him, too. Except she was the kind of freedom he could never really have.

Although he'd been avoiding this conversation with her for days—if he was being honest with himself, maybe he'd been avoiding it for two years—he suddenly wanted her to know, to understand him. "I don't remember them. I've seen my file—apparently public safety officers found me locked in a closet and emaciated—but I don't remember that, either."

Tears filled her eyes, and her lips started trembling, trying to hold them back.

He gave her a small smile. "It's okay. I honestly have no memory of that time."

She clutched his hand tighter. "It doesn't matter," she said, sounding furious on his behalf. "It's still part of you, whether you consciously remember it or not. It's not okay."

"No. But I just—I never had a normal family. I don't know anything else. Until Andre and Marcos came along, it was just me. And—"

"And even then you wanted to take care of them."

"Yeah." The tightness in his chest loosened a little, knowing she understood.

"So then who looks after you?"

A smile quirked his lips. "Nobody needs to anymore. I got through that time. And now I'm an adult. I'm a cop."

"Right. So you can take care of even more people."

He'd never thought of it that way, but he supposed it was true. Still… "What's wrong with that?"

"Nothing." She smiled at him, but it was sad. "But everyone needs someone to look after them."

He didn't like the idea of her feeling sorry for him, and he shifted on the bed, pulling away from her a little. "I don't think—"

The ringing of his phone cut him off. Cole used his free hand to pull it out of his pocket, not wanting to completely sever the connection to Shaye yet. He glanced down. Luke.

Pressing the phone to his ear, he answered. "What's up?"

"We found the car."

"Good." Except why did Luke's voice sound dire?

"No, not good, Cole. We've confirmed that it's what Dominic drove to the station—he parked a few blocks away—but it's not right."

"Not right how?" Cole asked as a bad feeling came over him, suspecting what Luke was going to say next.

"It's not the same car. Dominic isn't the one who was shooting at Shaye. Whoever was trying to kill her is still out there."

Chapter Eleven

"Are we sure it's not Dominic?" Cole asked. "Maybe he just used a different car when he followed Shaye in the police vehicle. We never did find what he was driving when he hit Roy's Grocery."

Cole stared hopefully at his partner, but inside he was discouraged. He'd come to the station an hour ago after personally dropping Shaye at the lab next door and forbidding her to leave until he came to get her. It was mid-morning on Monday, but he figured her boss would cut her a little slack after what she'd been through.

"Pretty sure," Luke replied, somehow looking wide-awake despite how little sleep Cole knew he'd had all weekend. His partner sat ramrod straight at his desk, managing to radiate authority despite the cargo pants and T-shirt their boss was always trying to get him to stop wearing. "The car is a really old Taurus, just like the one at Shaye's shooting, but it's the wrong color. And according to Hiroshi, it's way less of a rust bucket than the vehicle that was following his patrol car."

"And the one you found is definitely the car Crazy Ed left to Rosa?"

"Yep. The VIN matches."

"Do we know where Dominic was keeping it yet? Because I'm not ready to drop this guy yet. He sure looked like the shooter, wearing another hoodie at the scene."

"A hoodie isn't exactly a smoking gun," Luke countered. "And Dominic had a semiautomatic, whereas Shaye's shooter was carrying a standard pistol. Why the difference?"

"I'm a cop. He'd expect me to be armed. I'm sure he figured Shaye would be an easy target." The idea made his whole body tense. He'd tried so hard last year to clean up the Jannis Crew—in large part because it was his job and they'd killed three of his coworkers. But also because he knew Shaye would never truly be safe if he didn't get all of them.

The fact that she was still dodging bullets made him wish he'd pushed harder for Witness Protection last year. Except then she'd be out of his life for good, and even thinking about that was painful.

"Maybe." Luke still didn't sound convinced. "Until Dominic wakes up—*if* he wakes up— all we've got is the car. And the other gang members, but they're not talking. They're clearly more afraid of their leader's wrath than doing serious jail time."

"Like he can't get to them in prison." Cole scowled, debating whether another interview was worthwhile.

"On the upside," Luke said, "we found Rosa and Ed Jr."

"Really?" Cole whirled his desk chair toward his partner. "Where?"

"They went to stay with her older sister out in the suburbs. It's not the best hiding place, but I talked to her on the phone right before you got in. She said her brother told her to take off last night. Claims she didn't know why, but she had a feeling he'd gotten wrapped up in something bad just like her ex used to, and so she did. She also says Dominic was trying to get out of the Kings. She thought that's why he wanted her gone."

"Hmm. If that's true, the other gang members coming after him might not be about him trying to kill a cop without permission.

It might just be because he's trying to leave the group."

"Yeah. I'm not sure that should make Rosa feel any safer, but she claims Leonardo and Crazy Ed had an understanding, and that because of it, Leonardo would never come after her or the kid."

"Leonardo?"

Luke laughed. "Yeah, not exactly the kind of name you'd expect a gang leader to have, right?"

Cole nodded, trying to shake off thoughts of Shaye. Of course he knew the name of the Kings' leader. He needed to get his head in the game. "So you believe Rosa when she says she didn't know what Dominic planned to do last night? What did she say when you asked about him going after Shaye?"

"Well, I talked to her on the phone, so it's not like I could watch her body language. But yeah, I believe her. And she didn't even seem to know who Shaye was. Which makes me think Dominic wasn't the one trying to kill her."

Cole frowned. If Dominic had been looking for revenge on his sister's behalf, it didn't make a lot of sense that Rosa didn't know Shaye's name. Unless she was a good liar. Or Dominic's grudge went deeper than hers, which he could imagine. Because although he was furious about being shot at last night, he was more angry at himself for letting it happen than at the men who'd come after him. But when he thought about Andre coming under fire earlier this year by his girlfriend's ex, Cole sure had a lot of fury for that crook.

"I'm not ready to give up on Dominic yet. But you're right. We need to broaden our search again." Cole tapped his fingers on his desk, out of brilliant ideas. They'd gone through the list of people with possible grudges against Shaye. And they'd gone through the evidence from the shooting at Roy's Grocery. Neither had yielded anything.

"I'm not sure where—" Luke started when an idea bloomed and Cole cut him off.

"You said the Kings' leader was anxious to convince us he had nothing to do with this, right?"

Luke swore, long and creatively until Cole had to laugh. His partner knew him well enough to realize Cole was about to suggest something dangerous.

"Now you sound like a sailor," Cole joked.

Luke flipped him off with a smile that quickly turned serious. "I'm not going to like this, am I?"

"Probably not."

"Okay, lay it on me."

"I think we should go talk to the head of the Kings gang."

There was a long pause; then Luke finally

demanded, "Are you crazy? Didn't we *just* talk about you trying to stay out of the line of fire?"

"Yeah, and I plan to."

"By scheduling a meet-up with a gang leader?"

"Look, you said it yourself. Leonardo was desperate to convince you that he had nothing to do with this. Let's see if we can get him to tell us what those other gang members were doing there."

Luke didn't budge from his seat, just crossed his arms over his chest. "You think he'd tell us if he ordered a hit on anyone?"

"No. But I think he's seen how dogged we can be, what we did with the Jannis Crew. I think he'll find a way to tell us what we need to know without admitting anything."

Luke scowled, but Cole could tell his argument was making sense to his partner. "Because then we'll know if we have to worry whether Dominic has any other friends willing to take up his cause."

"Yeah. And given the way things went down last night, if Leonardo suspects who they are, I think he'll hand those names over fast."

Luke swore again and opened his top drawer, pulling out his weapon and holstering it. "All right, but let's be really careful how we handle this. I don't want a repeat of last night."

"Believe me," Cole muttered as he followed Luke out to the car. "Neither do I."

"HI, SHAYE."

It took Shaye a minute to identify the voice on the phone, but then she realized. "Andre. Is Cole okay?"

Panic struck as she glanced in the direction of the police station, so close. Could something have happened without her hearing about it? She *was* pretty insulated, way in the back by herself in her closet of a lab. She jumped to her feet.

"Yeah, he's fine."

Shaye let out a long breath. "Good."

"Sorry. I didn't mean to worry you. I was just checking in with you."

In the background, she heard a strange *whomp whomp whomp* she couldn't identify. "What is that? Where are you?"

"Quantico. Just came down from a helicopter and I had a sec, so I wanted to make sure everything was all right there. Nothing out of the ordinary at the lab?"

"No." Just a handful of new digital devices she needed to analyze, and then hope the results wouldn't send a criminal after her. Shaking off the negativity, she asked, "Did Cole tell you to call?"

"No. But I know he doesn't like having you out of eyesight, and my brother's worry tends to rub off on me, even when it's unnecessary."

He laughed, and she could tell it was for her benefit. "Inside a forensics lab fifty yards away from a police station is pretty safe."

Except for last year. Or last night.

Of course, both of those incidents had taken place in the parking lot, so she should be fine as long as she stayed in here. The lab required a key card to get in, not just at the front door but also at each lab. And no one had the card to access her room except for her and the director.

She'd been jumpy all day—she didn't like being away from Cole, either, and it was from worrying about his safety as much as her own—but she forced her voice to sound unconcerned. "Everything is fine here."

"Great," Andre said, sounding rushed now. "Listen, I've got to go back up and rappel out of the copter again. But be safe and tell Cole I'll talk to him tonight."

Andre was gone before she could say goodbye. Shaye stared down at the phone for a minute, bemused and touched. Cole might not have had a traditional family—or any family—for too many years, but he sure did now. He cared about her, so his brothers did, too.

She almost laughed when her phone rang again and it was Marcos. "Hi, Marcos. I just got off a call with your brother."

"What's Cole up to right now? Any new leads?"

"Your other brother."

"Oh." Marcos laughed. "Guess we think alike. I suppose you already told him everything is fine there, right? You're safe?"

"I'm good." She paused, biting her lip, wondering if she could talk to Marcos about what had kept her distracted all morning.

"Out with it," Marcos said. "What's worrying you? Because I promise you Cole is going to keep you safe."

"No, it's not that." She absolutely believed

Cole would do everything in his power to make certain nothing happened to her. The question was whether something would happen to *him* in the process. "I just… Cole told me a little bit about the fire that happened when you were kids, but we got interrupted and he never said how you all managed to make it out of there." A terrible thought occurred to her. "Did someone get stuck inside?"

There was a long pause, and Shaye realized she'd probably just crossed a boundary, asking Cole's brother for personal details he hadn't yet shared with her himself. "I'm sorry. I—"

"That's okay." Marcos sounded more subdued than usual. "I guess I shouldn't be surprised he told you about the fire, but Cole keeps stuff to himself. Honestly, I'm not sure he's really talked about it to anyone besides us and Luke."

Oh, Cole. Sadness slumped her shoulders,

thinking how few people Cole let into his world. And it was such an incredible world.

"We all got out. The fire started downstairs, and the kids were all upstairs. Well, almost all of us," he amended and she could tell there was a story there, but he kept going. "I woke up and it was like being blind from the smoke. I couldn't breathe, couldn't see, didn't know what was happening or what to do. I was twelve."

There was another pause, and Shaye knew she was making Marcos relive it. She opened her mouth to tell him it was okay, that he didn't have to tell her, when he continued.

"Then Cole was there, waking up Andre, making us hold on to each other as we went down the stairs. I don't know what happened, but I tripped and then they were gone." He let out a loud breath. "Scariest moment of my life. But I managed to make it out. And by the time I got outside, it was clear the whole place was about to go up. Cole was holding Andre back, but if he hadn't… I guarantee you, they both would have run back in for me. And it would have been a bad idea. I had to go another way."

Shaye took a shaky breath, realizing she'd been holding it while Marcos spoke, even though she knew they'd all lived through the fire. "And after that you were all separated?"

"Yeah. Those foster parents had to rebuild, so they didn't have a place for us anymore. It was hard not having Andre and Cole around all the time, although we tried to find ways to talk, to see each other if we could. But let me tell you, the minute I turned eighteen, Cole was there, waiting on the doorstep." Marcos's voice sounded teary as he finished. "He had a home waiting for me."

"He's a great guy," Shaye said, her own voice watery. She knew he'd supported Andre and

Marcos when they'd gotten out of foster care; he'd accidentally shared as much with her a few days ago. It shouldn't have surprised her that he'd literally been standing outside to drive Marcos home when he hit eighteen and the foster system kicked him out to make it on his own.

"Yeah, he is. And I know he can be hard to reach sometimes—or at least it might seem that way—but he's worth sticking it out for, Shaye."

"I…" What could she say to that? That Cole didn't want her in his life, at least not that way? That she was scared even if he did, she wasn't cut out to date someone who put his life on the line as part of his job description?

"Just don't give up on him," Marcos said softly. "I've got to go, Shaye. I've got an undercover meet in less than an hour, and I'm going to be late."

"I'm sorry. I—"

"Stay safe. Tell Cole I'll call him."

"Okay," Shaye promised, but he was already gone.

And then she was staring at the wall in her lab, covered with cartoons only someone with a deep understanding of digital analysis would find funny, but not really seeing any of them. She'd known it all along, but Marcos's words had just driven it home. Cole deserved someone in his life, someone who would look after him as much as he looked after everyone around him. And he deserved someone much, much braver than she could ever hope to be.

Chapter Twelve

The second Cole parked his car alongside the curb, six men wearing gang colors and shirts loose enough to cover weapons started ambling his way.

"Maybe we should rethink this," Luke muttered from the passenger seat, his hand hovering near his own weapon on his hip. His gaze scanned the area.

Before Cole could reconsider, there was a yell, and the men all stopped, glanced over their shoulders and then walked back the way they'd come. Then just one man was walking toward them, his hands out at his sides, to show he wasn't holding.

"Leonardo," Luke muttered, opening his door.

Cole followed, walking around the front of the car as he inspected the leader of the Kings. Leonardo Carrera was a big guy, at least 250 and only five-ten. He was covered in tattoos, with a seemingly permanent scowl on his face. He'd had a handful of run-ins with the law, but despite having a reputation as a man not to cross in the gang world, he tended not to mess around with law enforcement, especially since the Jannis Crew had been shut down.

"Detectives," he greeted them now, as if he were an upstanding citizen welcoming them into his home instead of a gangster who'd ordered hits on men—if only they could prove it.

"Leonardo." Cole's gaze assessed the other Kings members. "Can we have a little chat in private?"

Leonardo glanced over his shoulder and nodded, and the other men scattered, some heading inside the house behind them and others striding down the street. "Of course. What can I do for you?"

Talking to the head of the Kings always threw Cole, and he remembered that Leonardo had actually gotten a business degree before returning to his old neighborhood and taking over the gang his older brother had run before his death a few years earlier. It was probably why the Kings were so good at making money—and had been so successful at evading law enforcement. That would eventually change. Just not today.

Today Cole had other concerns on his mind.

"I need some information about Dominic Elliard," Cole told Leonardo.

"He's not a part of my social circle anymore," Leonardo said.

Normally Leonardo's euphemisms would make Cole smile, but today he just scowled. "And when did that happen?"

Leonardo shrugged. "It's been coming for a while. I knew he wanted out, and that's just not cool with me. Let one guy leave and others think they can do the same if they feel like it. But I was gonna make an exception and let him go, seeing how he's looking after his sister and all."

"You and Ed have some kind of agreement?" Luke asked.

Leonardo gave a smile that was somehow far more creepy than happy. "Let's just say we understood each other. We grew up together. He chose the wrong side. Obviously. But we were good friends once." The smile dropped off. "A long time ago. So, yeah, I was giving Dominic a little leeway, for Ed's sake. But then he started talking about revenge on cops, and I'm not having any part of that. I'm a businessman, you know."

Cole nodded, knowing Leonardo actually

thought that. "When did this come up, Dominic's plan to get revenge on cops?"

"Yesterday."

"Yesterday?" Cole glanced over at Luke, who was frowning. They'd visited Dominic for the first time yesterday, but Shaye had been shot at before that. "What about shooting lab employees?"

"Lab?" Leonardo shook his head, looking perplexed. "What kind of lab?"

"County forensics," Luke said.

"Didn't come up. It was cops. He said they visited Rosa's place, talking smack about taking her car, and it brought up all this old anger." Leonardo paused, glanced from him to Luke. "Guess that was you two, huh? Dominic thought he was going to get all of Ed's money when he went to jail or after he died, like it wouldn't get caught up in the system. Fool. He never got over that. It's been stewing inside of him for a year."

"What about the others who were at the police station last night?" Luke asked, taking a step toward Leonardo that made the gangster raise an eyebrow. He shifted slightly backward at the force of Luke's glare. Leonardo might have had a solid seventy pounds on Luke and probably more than one pistol hidden on his massive body, but Luke had seen some serious combat as a Marine that still showed when he wanted it to.

"Shouldn't have happened where it did," Leonardo said, speaking slowly, like he was choosing every word carefully.

Which he surely was, since any obvious admission to participation in a crime would land him in a jail cell. And knowledge of it before it happened could land him in cuffs, too.

"So, they were interested in Dominic?" Luke pressed.

"Yeah. They were supposed to...talk him out of whatever he planned to do." He gave a toothy smile. "I don't stand for people who step out of line, you know."

"We've heard that," Cole said. He believed the man. "Thanks for your time."

As he and Luke turned to go back to their car, Leonardo called, "I heard about that shooting at the grocery store. Papers said a county employee was hit. That what you're interested in?"

Cole spun back. "You know anything about it?"

Leonardo held up his hands. "All I can tell you is it wasn't anyone from my social group. Not my, uh, chess opponents, either."

Cole stared at him, knowing he was referring to members of other area gangs. "How sure are you?"

"About my own? Positive. About the others? Pretty sure. If it was them, I'd have heard about it by now. Someone would have bragged. Word always gets out about that kind of thing."

Cole nodded and returned to the car. Instead of starting it up, he looked over at Luke as his partner climbed in and slammed the door. "You believe him?"

"That no gang member was behind this? Yeah. If it was gang related, someone went way off the reservation."

Cole ground his teeth together as he started the engine, resisting the urge to repeat some of the creative cursing Luke had done earlier. If it wasn't a gang member, then they were down to zero suspects in the attempt on Shaye's life, and she was still in danger.

COLE WAS IN a bad mood when he met Shaye in her lab at the end of her workday.

Actually, it was two hours past the end of her workday, but she didn't mind. She knew he was trying to confirm Dominic Elliard was the one who'd shot at her, and she had plenty to catch up on anyway. Being away from the lab for a year—even though they'd sent digital devices to the state lab in the meantime—meant there had been a lot waiting for her when she returned. They'd tried to ease her back in with just a few assignments, but today, she'd asked for everything.

"What's wrong?" Shaye asked Cole, nerves rising up because she knew before he spoke that the investigation wasn't closed.

Cole's shoulders slumped. "I'm sorry, but it doesn't look like Dominic Elliard is our shooter."

"What?" That didn't make any sense. "I thought you arrested him at the scene?"

"No, I mean, yes, we did. He's *my* shooter, but he's not the one who was coming after you. We'll still talk to him when he wakes up, but I think there's someone else out there."

"Then why was Dominic shooting at you if it's not connected? I thought you talked to him about the attempt on me, and that's why he came after you?"

"Sort of." Cole sighed. "Turns out, Dominic was pissed about Ed's money and belongings being confiscated."

"But he earned them illegally—"

"Yeah, I know, but Dominic thought it all should have gone to his sister—or directly to him, for some reason. When we asked about the car, I guess that was the last straw. He snapped."

Shaye tried to wrap her mind around that. "Are you serious? He shot up a police station over a rusted-out, decade-old car?"

"Seems so."

She shifted from one foot to the other, wrapping her arms around herself to ward off a sudden chill. "What does this mean for me?" Before he could speak, she added, "Please don't say Witness Protection."

She might not see her family as often as she'd

like to since she'd moved here, but never seeing them again? She couldn't even imagine it. And the thought of never seeing Cole again hurt just as badly. Whatever the threat was, she couldn't give up the people she loved to stop it. Not even if it meant her own life was in danger.

Loved. The word rolled around in her brain as she realized she'd put Cole in the same category as her family. But she couldn't dwell on that now, because she had bigger concerns than falling for a detective who'd never feel the same.

This was never going to end. The fear. Never knowing if she was safe or if she'd walk outside and face a barrage of bullets. Was this what Cole felt like every day as a detective? "How do you do this?"

"Do what?" he asked, peeling her hands off her arms and holding them in his. "Listen, I'm sorry it's not over. I wanted this to be the end of it. But we're not giving up until whoever did this is in handcuffs. Until then I'm going to keep you safe. I promise you, Shaye."

"How do you deal with this without going crazy, without being too paralyzed to live?"

"The danger?" he asked softly, something in his eyes shifting, though she wasn't sure if it was worry or pity for her or just Cole closing himself off.

"Yeah. Because you just seem to run into it like it's nothing. I don't know how to do that. I don't know how—"

"You don't *have* to do that. I don't want you doing that. I'm going to get this guy, Shaye, whoever he is, and then things can go back to normal."

She didn't want them to go back to normal. Frustration filled her, almost overtaking the fear. She wanted to learn how to manage the fear. She wanted to understand the risks that

Cole faced, so she could stop feeling so terrified whenever he was out of her sight.

Shaye sank into her chair, not letting go of Cole's hands. When had this happened? When had her worry about Cole become greater than her concerns about the threat facing her? She dropped her head on top of their hands.

When had she gone from halfway in love with him to totally, madly, completely in love? And what the heck was she going to do about it?

"I STILL DON'T like this," Cole said an hour later as he opened the door and tucked her under his arm, practically running her to the hospital entrance.

"Maybe if I see him, it'll spark something."

"And maybe if he sees her, it will be obvious he recognizes her," Luke added as he met them in the lobby.

"All right," Cole grumbled. "Let's get this

over with. I want Shaye back in a controlled location. There are too many people here."

"This guy would have to be pretty desperate to try and shoot up a hospital," Luke said.

"Yeah, well, Elliard shot up a police station," Cole reminded him.

Luke gave Shaye a look she interpreted as "my partner is seriously overreacting," and she gave a hesitant smile in return.

Since her realization in the lab, she'd felt completely distracted and way too self-conscious, like Cole would read her mind. It wasn't totally unreasonable—she'd seen him pick up on things people were thinking plenty of times. It must have been part of his detective skill set. She didn't want him using it on her. Not today.

He'd definitely known something was wrong that she wasn't sharing, though, because he'd asked her about it the entire ride over here after Luke had called to tell them Dominic Elliard had woken up. Thankfully, he'd seemed to think it was just fear of not having her shooter in custody. She was perfectly happy to let him keep thinking that until she figured out what she was going to do about her feelings for him.

"Come on," Luke said, leading the way over to the elevator. "He's been moved out of ICU. But I didn't give him a heads-up we'd be coming, and given that he just regained consciousness, we'd better be careful if we ask him anything we expect to need in a courtroom."

"We've got him on the police station shooting no matter what," Cole said. "Our cameras caught him pretty clearly, plus my testimony. But we'll need to be careful how we approach Shaye's shooting. If he actually did do that, I want him going away for it, too."

Luke nodded. "Agreed. Though the reality is that unless someone majorly screws up here, this guy shouldn't ever get out."

The elevator reached the third floor, and the three of them headed down the hall. An officer stood outside a room that had to be Dominic's. Cole and Luke exchanged a few words with the officer, and then Shaye took a deep breath as they opened the hospital door.

She didn't think she'd seen the shooter's face at the scene, but she knew that sometimes witnesses recalled more than they thought they did when faced with a lineup. Would she recognize Dominic?

She followed Cole and Luke into the room and stared at the man in the hospital room. He was unnaturally pale, with a bandage covering the right half of his chest, his arm in a sling and a bunch of tubes and wires connected to him.

He turned his head slowly, wincing, and his lips turned up into a snarl when he spotted them.

Shaye studied him, her heart thudding too rapidly, taking in the exaggerated cupid's bow of his lips, the small eyes with the heavy eyebrows, the thin nose that had clearly been broken at least once. His focus shifted off Cole and Luke over to her, and he met her gaze.

He had dark brown eyes. They looked angry and a little confused. But she didn't recognize them. She didn't recognize him. She let out a nervous breath, then glanced over at Cole and shook her head.

"Let me guess," Dominic said, obviously going for a sarcastic tone but failing when it came out weak. "You came here to get my car keys."

"Actually, Dominic, we found your car already," Luke said. "We came here to talk to you about Shaye."

"Who?"

"Shaye." Cole gestured to her, and Dominic's gaze bounced back to her.

"I don't know who that is. You plan to give her my car?"

"It's not your car, Dominic. And you're probably not going to have much use for one in prison," Cole snapped. "So I'd cut the sarcasm and try to cooperate."

He rolled his eyes. "Cooperate with what? You said you already took my car."

"Forget the car," Luke said. "We want to talk to you about a shooting that happened three days ago."

Dominic let out a string of curses, his voice gaining strength with each one. "Oh, no. You're not pinning some random shooting on me. What's this? That gangbanger over on 109? That wasn't me. Why would I shoot him?"

"That's not who we're talking about, Dominic," Luke said. "We're talking about Shaye."

He looked confused for a minute. "She ain't shot."

Luke shook his head just as Dominic went into another rant about being framed. "Thanks for your time, Dominic," Luke said, gesturing for them to follow as he left the room.

"He didn't recognize her," Luke said.

"Yeah, and he definitely couldn't hide his anger toward us," Cole agreed, "but he seemed indifferent to Shaye. He's not our guy."

"So who is?" Shaye asked as they headed back to the elevator.

Dominic's cursing followed them the whole way.

Chapter Thirteen

"You've been acting weird all evening," Cole said, studying Shaye and trying to figure out what was going on with her. He knew she was worried about still being in danger, but all his detective instincts were screaming that there was more to it than that. "What's going on?"

Shaye fidgeted on his couch, still wearing the conservative gray slacks and emerald green blouse she'd worn to work. She'd knotted her hair up into a bun on top of her head, and it had loosened, looking like all it needed was a little tug from his fingers to send her hair cascading down.

He sat on the edge of the chair, keeping his distance, and stared at her. They were back at his house, where she was going to stay until this case was conclusively solved. The desire to have her here even longer nagged at him, but he needed to continue to remind himself to keep things professional. He hoped he could manage to do it.

"Nothing." She shrugged, her fingers twitching on the couch as she avoided his gaze. "It's just been a long day. Maybe we should order a pizza."

"Sure, but you honestly expect me to believe that?" He couldn't stop his grin. "I'm a detective, and you might just be the worst liar I've ever met."

Her gaze snapped to his, her lips parting at the insult, and he couldn't help but follow the move with his eyes. She didn't seem to wear lipstick, just swiped some pink gloss on her lips periodically that he desperately wanted to kiss right off.

Professional, he reminded himself.

"It's been a tough day," she said. "I'm just trying to…figure things out."

He instantly got serious. "I told you I'd protect you, Shaye, and I meant it."

"I know. It's not that. But…"

"What?"

"Who's going to keep *you* safe?"

He suddenly realized she looked truly worried. Her lips were actually trembling a little, and there was a sheen of tears over her whiskey-brown eyes.

"Hey." He got up from the chair and joined her on the couch, sitting far closer than he knew was wise. "Shaye, I had to go through a lot of training to be a cop. I might have joined because it would provide a good income without a real degree, but—"

"Bull."

"What?"

"You joined to keep people safe."

"Well, sure, that was part of the appeal, but I'm serious about the income. There aren't a lot of jobs that give you decent benefits *and* a decent salary with nothing but a high school degree, and being a cop is one of them." He felt himself flush, because he knew how smart she was, but he was mad at himself for doing it. He had a good job and he'd done what he needed to do to take care of the people he loved. He shouldn't feel ashamed about that.

"And you needed *that* because you were planning to take care of Marcos and Andre," Shaye said, sounding pleased with herself.

"Sure." He shrugged. "So? What does this have to do with anything? Look, the city gives us solid training, and I have one of the best partners on the force. You know Luke always has my back."

"Marcos told me about the fire, about how you got them both out," Shaye said, biting her lip as she stared up at him.

"He did?" She nodded, and he wasn't sure if it surprised him or not. His brothers were more open about their past than he tended to be. But how had the conversation come back to this? "Okay. And you're bringing that up because?"

"Because I want to know about you. I want to understand how you keep safe in your job, and I want to know about your past. I want…"

She was silent for so long that he finally prompted, "What? What do you want, Shaye?"

"You."

His heart picked up speed, like he'd gotten a sudden jolt of adrenaline the way he did when a case came together. Only this was much more potent.

Shaye Mallory wanted *him*. He stared at her, at the hopeful, nervous expression on her face, and gripped the couch cushion to keep from grabbing her and yanking her to him. Because he didn't think he'd ever wanted anything as badly as he wanted her right now.

He cared about her. A lot. And he knew Shaye. She wasn't the fling sort. She hadn't dated anyone—not even casually—during the entire time she'd worked at the lab. And it wasn't like she hadn't had opportunities. He'd heard colleagues ask her out, watched her blush and stammer and try to let them down easy. Shaye wasn't the kind of woman you messed around with, and he sure wasn't going to be the one to break her heart.

He was always going to be a blue-collar guy, a first responder who ran toward all the things she should stay far away from. He tried to calm his pulse and let her down as easy as she had all those other guys. "Shaye—"

"I know you're attracted to me."

He let out a heavy breath. "Yeah, of course I am, but—"

"And I know you like me as a person. You'd be good for me, Cole. And you know what? I think I'd be good for you."

His heart pinched at the idea of rejecting her. She looked so nervous and so determined. But in the long run, he was doing her a favor. Probably himself, too. How did anyone get over Shaye Mallory?

"Shaye, we're really different."

"Who cares?" He tried to talk, but she kept going, speaking fast so he couldn't break in without talking over her. She leaned even closer, challenging his resolve as she said, "You have a high school degree. I have a bachelor's and a master's. Who cares?"

She had multiple degrees? That shouldn't surprise him.

"You grew up in foster care, and I grew up with a big Irish Catholic family that drives me crazy because they're so loud and busy and outgoing, and I'm just not. Who cares? You're a cop, and I sit in front of computers all day. Who cares? All that really matters is that I…" She took a deep breath, blew it out and looked at her shoes before staring up at him. "Cole, I—"

He cut her off before she said anything she'd really regret, before she said anything that made him either put someone else on her protection detail or drag her into his arms and never let go. "*I* care, Shaye—that's who. Those differences matter to me. We're not a good fit. We never will be. I'm sorry."

SHAYE WAS DREADING seeing Cole this morning. She'd mumbled something about being tired last night after he'd rejected her like he didn't even need to give it any thought and then she'd run off to his guest room.

The relative solitude hadn't helped, because the room looked like Cole, all masculine and practical. Somehow it smelled like him, too. Maybe she was just imagining his scent, conjuring it up to torture herself.

She'd put herself on the line, been about to

admit she loved him—which surely he'd realized—and he'd said no so easily. Her cheeks flushed just thinking about how badly she'd embarrassed herself. The worst part was she didn't understand it. He was attracted to her; that had been obvious not just in the kisses they'd shared but in the way he looked at her when he thought she wouldn't notice. And he liked her—they'd become friends almost instantly. It should have been enough. Enough at least to give something more a *chance*.

But apparently not for Cole.

And now she had to go sit across the kitchen table from him and eat breakfast, then let him drive her to the lab. Then he'd pick her up at the end of the day and drive her back here for another awkward evening together. And there was no end in sight, no real suspects in her case now that they'd ruled out Elliard.

She needed to do something. Review the cases she'd worked on herself, double-check everything, then make a list of anyone in her life. She couldn't imagine any of her colleagues doing this, but working in law enforcement had taught her that people could surprise you. Maybe if she ran down leads, too, this would end sooner. She'd be able to go back home, and go back to her old life. Problem was she didn't want her old life anymore.

She wanted something better. She wanted to get the joy in her job back, sure, but she wanted to have a life outside the lab, too. Most of all she wanted Cole. But she couldn't have him, so she needed to take charge of the things she could control. And this was a good place to start.

"Shaye?" Cole's voice was more tentative than she'd ever heard it. It was followed by a few taps on the bedroom door. "You ready to go?"

"Yep." She grabbed her purse, straightened her shoulders and pulled open the door.

There wasn't much she could do about the blush she felt making her whole face hot, but she tilted her chin up and strode toward his front door. "Let's go."

He followed, wisely not saying a word until he dropped her off at the lab and promised to pick her up at the end of the day.

As the lab door swung closed behind her, she tried not to dwell on the heaviness in her heart. Despite the fact that they'd never really interacted socially, Cole had become one of the best friends she had. Her declaration last night had ruined that.

She was going to miss what they'd had. But she still couldn't bring herself to regret trying for more. It was time to start doing that in all aspects of her life.

If she didn't get what she wanted, at least she'd go down with a fight.

"GET YOUR HEAD in the game." Luke slapped a rolled-up stack of papers against his arm, and Cole scowled back.

"Focus, man. You've been distracted all day."

"Sorry." He tried for the millionth time to shake off thoughts of last night. Had Shaye really been about to say what he'd thought? He'd gone over it in his head again and again and decided he was crazy. She couldn't possibly love him—or think she loved him. If that *had* been what she was going to say, it was probably just a result of their close proximity. Having your life in danger made you think and say all kinds of crazy things.

"I think we need to focus on the car again," Luke announced. From the way he said it, Cole suspected he'd been repeating it.

Cole straightened in his chair, let the sounds of the bullpen filter back in: the ridiculously old coffeepot gurgling in the corner, the old pipes rattling, a group of officers talking about traffic-stop safety in the corner. It helped him focus, but he still didn't have any brilliant new ideas. "Without a license plate, I'm not sure how far an old, rusty Taurus is going to get us."

"Let's go back to that list of suspects you made, of people connected to Shaye's case. I don't care if the person has an alibi—let's run them all and see what they drive. Because Dominic isn't the only one who could be on a vengeance mission for someone else."

New energy filled Cole. "You're right. But wouldn't the person drive their own car?"

"Yeah," Luke agreed. "So we're going to be looking at a lot of names, but unless you have another idea…"

"Nope. Let's do it. And while we're at it, let's just see what her colleagues are driving. I doubt any of them have a grudge no one knows about, but stalkers are usually in the person's life, even if they're way in the periphery, so let's check."

Two hours later, Cole looked up from the records he'd been cross-referencing on his computer and rubbed eyes that had long since gone blurry.

"Here."

He looked up and found Luke holding out a cup of coffee. "Thanks." Cole took a big sip, hoping to erase some of the fog from not sleeping last night. Or the night before. Or any night, really, since Shaye had been shot at in a parking lot.

"You want to tell me what's eating at you?" Luke asked, leaning against the edge of Cole's desk and effectively preventing him from diving right back into the search.

"You know what's bothering me. It's this whole case. I don't like seeing Shaye in danger."

"Nah." Luke sipped his coffee leisurely and settled in more comfortably against Cole's desk. "We've been partners long enough. We've been *friends* long enough. I know there's more to it. And I know you're not big on sharing your feelings, and I get it, but come on. You look like you could use a sounding board."

Was he really that bad? Cole frowned at his partner, weighing the things Shaye had said to him over the past few days about not letting anyone close to him. "Shaye's said some things lately. Do I really keep everyone at arm's length?"

"Yeah." There wasn't even a brief pause while Luke considered it. "But, look, we're all like that at least a little. It's a cop's nature, I think. We spend so much time investigating all the horrible things people do to each other, all the ways they betray one another." He shrugged. "We're bound to get a little jaded."

But Cole had always been this way. And he might have had reason, but that didn't mean it was a good way to live.

He set down the coffee and leaned back in his chair, thinking about all the times Shaye had tried to get to know him better the past few days and all the ways he'd tried to push her away. Maybe they were too different to ever make something last. But if she was crazy enough to want to give someone like him a chance, then how much crazier was he not to take it?

Maybe it was time to make some real changes in his life. And maybe he needed to start with Shaye Mallory.

Chapter Fourteen

"Shaye." Cole let out a string of swearwords as she walked toward him.

Shaye kept her head up and tried not to let the sight of him hurt but failed miserably. She had no idea how she was going to get over this man, but solving this case so she wasn't under his roof was probably a good start.

"What are you doing here? What's wrong? Why didn't you call me? I would have come and gotten you."

"I walked across the parking lot," Shaye cut in before Cole could continue his barrage of questions. "I'm fine. There were four officers standing outside the whole time."

His lips pinched together, and she could tell he was letting it go even though he wasn't appeased. "What's wrong?"

"Nothing's wrong. I had some information I thought you might want." She'd been digging up information all day on her tablet—thank goodness she'd brought her personal one so she didn't have to do this on her work computer. She was now behind on what she *should* have been doing at work today, but she just might be one step closer to figuring out who was after her.

"Okay, let's hear it," Cole said, standing up and offering her his chair as Luke rolled his chair around the desk to join them.

Shaye settled into the seat, still warm from Cole's body, and dang it, even the chair smelled like him. She scooted forward a little, trying to focus and glanced up, catching his gaze. And then everything—her breathing, her thoughts, her very heartbeat—seemed to jerk to a stop, then start up again in double time.

Cole was staring at her with a look she'd never seen before. He'd looked at her with desire in the past, but usually it was tempered, like he was trying to hide it. Right now it was like he was intentionally broadcasting that he wanted her. His gaze drifted slowly over her, then back up, with lingering eye contact that made her squirm.

What was happening?

"Ahem." Luke coughed.

Cole gave her a slow smile, then blinked, and his serious detective face was back, and Shaye tried to decide if she'd just imagined the whole thing. Because those were some serious mixed signals, less than twenty-four hours after he'd told her they were too different to be together.

"What's the information?" Luke's voice seemed to come from far away. She must have taken a really long time to respond, because he added, "Shaye?"

"Um, right." She fussed with the hem of her shirt, pretending to straighten it as she tried to make her face blank as easily as Cole had done. Sure she was failing completely, but knowing she could only stall so long, she cleared her throat and said, "I want you guys to take a closer look at Ken Tobek."

"The engineer who tried to kill his wife?" Luke frowned. "He was alibied at the time of the shooting."

"By a friend, right?"

"Yeah, why?" Cole leaned toward her. "You have some new reason to suspect him? Did you remember something more from the day of the shooting?"

"No, but his brother-in-law owns a really old Taurus, along with a couple other vehicles. And the day of the shooting, he blew through a red light about five minutes away from Roy's

Grocery. It was earlier in the day," she rushed on, "so it doesn't ruin his alibi, but maybe he was casing the place, knowing I usually get my groceries before the weekend starts."

"And you know this how exactly?" Luke asked.

"We don't want to know," Cole said quickly, glancing around like he was making sure no one had overheard.

He knew her hacking capabilities very well, because she'd used them for Andre when his girlfriend had been in danger. She smiled, trying to look innocent.

"Okay, we'll look into it," Cole promised. "But I want you to stay away from this case."

"I—"

"And if you're not locked in that lab, I want you in my sight." His tone was firm, almost angry, and intense. "No exceptions, and I don't care how many police officers are nearby—

you got it? If they're not me or Luke, they don't count."

Luke laughed into the silence that followed. "Don't worry, Shaye. This is just Cole's way of saying you're important to him."

She expected Cole to scowl at his partner and walk her back to the lab. Instead he leaned close to her and whispered in her ear, his breath feathering across her skin. "He's right."

"PLEASE TELL ME Shaye hasn't been using her hacking skills to help us in investigations," Luke said.

Cole looked over at his partner and smiled. Most of their colleagues would probably assume Luke—the former Marine with the deadly stare who refused to wear anything but cargos and T-shirts to work—would be the rule bender. The reality was, of the two of them, Cole was more likely to use…unconventional methods. "No. But I knew she could do it. I asked her to help me out with a personal matter before, so I wasn't surprised."

"And by personal matter, you mean the hit men out to get Andre's girlfriend?" Luke asked, pulling their car to a stop at the curb in front of Ken Tobek's house.

"We weren't really worried about the chain of evidence," Cole replied, "so much as saving her life."

Luke nodded. "I hear you. But make sure Shaye watches her own trail. She should know better than anyone that if it's digital, it's traceable."

"Yeah, I know. I didn't ask her to do this one. I wouldn't have asked with Andre's case, but—"

"I get it. There were some strange circumstances there. But let's do this one by the book. We catch the person who's been coming after Shaye, and I want to be able to lock him up, not have him get out on an evidence technicality."

"Not a problem," Cole agreed, even though he didn't think he'd ever handled a case before this one where he honestly didn't care if the suspect ended up in handcuffs or a body bag.

He was way too emotionally invested. If he were really going by the book, he should recuse himself from the investigation because of a conflict of interest.

Cole grabbed Luke's arm as he started to open the door. "Don't say anything about my relationship with Shaye, okay? I don't want it getting out until this is over."

"Couldn't even if I wanted to," Luke replied. "Until you gave her bedroom eyes in the bullpen, I thought you were still being an idiot about the whole thing."

"I am," Cole muttered under his breath as Luke got out of the car. He should probably have been embarrassed by his partner's description, but he wasn't. He'd made his decision, and he'd needed to act on it before he chickened out. Even if he didn't deserve her, maybe he could make her happy for a while. And then hopefully the ultimate fall-out wouldn't destroy him.

It was ironic. He could run into gunfire, but he was scared to tell a woman how much he cared about her.

"You coming?" Luke called.

Cole climbed out of the car and followed his partner up the long drive to Tobek's house. The garage was shut, but there was a window. Cole took a quick detour to peer inside. "There's nothing in here but a Benz," he reported. "A new one."

"I just bought it."

The voice startled Cole, making his hand instinctively reach for his holster as he turned toward the voice.

"Why are you casing my place?" Tobek asked as he came around from the backyard, a pair of pruning shears in his hand. "Do I need to call the police?"

Luke flashed his badge. "We *are* the police. Could we come inside and talk to you for a few minutes, Mr. Tobek?"

The man stared at them a long minute, his lips pursed. He was the right build to be the shooter—average height and weight. He looked older than Cole remembered, his blond hair thinning, deep grooves under his eyes that a good night's sleep wasn't going to get rid of and horizontal lines from the corners of his lips downward, like he frowned often.

"You're the ones who arrested me and claimed I was trying to kill my wife." His voice was monotone, and Cole couldn't figure out if he'd just realized it or if he'd been pretending from the moment they'd showed up.

"Sir, we—" Luke started.

"I made a bad error in judgment that day. Got to drinking and let my anger get the best of me.

She frustrates me so much, and she wouldn't stop—" He let out a long breath. "But I would never have truly hurt her."

Cole made a noncommittal noise. The words of a man who was still blaming his ex-wife for his violence didn't hold a lot of weight in his book. But would the guy have come after Shaye? It seemed like a stretch. A coward like that seemed unlikely to chase after the forensics expert on his case while she was in the back of a police car.

But Shaye thought there could be something here, so he couldn't discount it. "We just have a few quick questions, and then we'll be on our way."

Tobek hefted the pruning shears, grabbing the handle a little higher, and used the long blades to point toward the backyard. "We can sit out back. I'll answer your questions, I guess, but you're not welcome in my house. I did jail time, and you two were part of that."

Cole gave Luke a perplexed glance as they followed him. For someone with obvious rage issues, Tobek was oddly calm. He'd expected more anger, more resistance to a discussion, not this bizarre monotone. But maybe Tobek was medicated—it might explain some things. Too bad Cole had no legitimate reason to go after that information.

A minute later, the three of them were settled at a huge wrought iron table that looked expensive and struck Cole as sort of sad, since the man now lived alone. But maybe he entertained a lot.

"We just want to ask you about last Friday night," Luke began.

"Are you kidding me?" Tobek snapped, then rolled his eyes. "Someone from the station already called about this. I mean, what exactly are you accusing me of?"

"We're not accusing you of anything," Cole said calmly, interested that this question had gotten a little emotion from the guy. "This is just a standard interview to knock you off a list."

Tobek's eyes narrowed. "What kind of list?"

"Someone came after a state employee, so we have to get alibis from anyone connected to her cases," Luke said. "So how about you help us out by giving us yours so we can move on?"

"I already did," Tobek said tightly, then settled back into his seat, as though he wanted them to think he didn't care they were questioning him again. "I had drinks with a guy from work, okay? I was at his place all evening. Check with him if you want."

"A friend of yours?" Cole asked.

Tobek shrugged. "Not really, no. But he's sort of new to the area, and he doesn't know a lot of people. He asked and I didn't want to be rude, so I said yes. To be honest, I think he asked a lot of people, but I guess I was the only one who agreed to go. It was a little last minute, and I happened to be free."

"What time did you get there? And what time did you leave?" Luke asked. "And did anyone else see you that night?"

"Jeez," Tobek said. "What is this? I need to make sure I'm around people all the time now because of one little mistake over a year ago? No, no one else saw me. I drove home after work, got home… I don't know, maybe six fifteen? Then I ate a quick dinner and I was at his place by seven thirty. I got home late, after midnight. The guy's a talker."

"What did you talk about?"

"What didn't we talk about? Work, life, women."

"What did you drive to his place?" Cole asked.

Tobek made a face. "You were just ogling it. My Mercedes. How many cars do you think I own?"

"Not an old Taurus?" Cole persisted, watching Tobek closely.

He squinted, shook his head, then spoke purposely slowly. "Why would I drive an old Taurus when I just bought a Mercedes?" He glanced at Luke, then back at Cole, and stood up. "Listen, I don't know what this is about—I don't even know your *state employee*—and I'm finished answering your bizarre questions. If you're fishing around, trying to get something on me, don't bother. I made one mistake. One. I paid my debt. It's over."

He pointed toward the front of the house, using the sharp end of the pruning shears he had clutched in his hand tightly enough to make his knuckles white. "Now get out."

SHE SHOULDN'T BE doing this.

Shaye glanced at the door again, even though she knew it was tightly shut. She was back in Cole's guest bedroom, but instead of Cole outside the room, it was Marcos. Cole had dropped her at his house after work, waited for Marcos to come and babysit her while he and Luke ran down her theory.

She felt a little bad about leaving Marcos to entertain himself when he was here keeping her safe, but an idea had struck on the drive back and refused to let go. So she'd claimed a headache and told Marcos she wanted to lie down for a while. His eyes had narrowed a little, like he could tell she was lying, but he'd simply nodded and let her go.

Now here she was, on her trusty tablet again, pulling up files she had no business accessing. But at least most of these were public record. This time, it wasn't so much that she was breaking the law to get information, more that she might be breaking Cole's trust.

He hadn't asked her to help him. But the words he'd spoken yesterday morning, when she'd woken up to him sitting on the edge of her bed had been haunting her ever since. *"I woke up and the house was on fire."* Then later in the conversation, he'd told her the fire had been ruled an accident. But the way he'd said it…

He didn't believe it.

And if someone had purposely set a house on fire with Cole and his brothers inside, she didn't care how many years it had been. She wanted answers for them.

Newspaper reports about the incident were surprisingly low on details: a house had burned to the ground around dawn. No one had died, but eight people had been inside at the time, including two adults and six foster kids, ranging in age from seventeen to eleven.

The images that went along with one of those reports made Shaye's heart ache for Cole. There were two shots: one where the fire was still in progress and firefighters were attempting to put it out, and another once the fire had been doused. The second one showed a shell of a home, burned out and totally unsalvageable. The first one showed flames seeming to shoot from the ground all the way up past the roof on the second story. She couldn't believe everyone had made it out of that fire.

She dug for information for another hour, then glanced at her closed door. If Marcos was anything like his older brother, he'd come check on her soon and make sure she was okay. Time to move on to less public records.

Thankfully, the fire department in the town where Cole had lived had digitized their old records, and their security was a joke. She pulled up the arson investigation report on the fire and read through it, frowning.

Point of origin had been a study on the first floor. Apparently candles had been left burning and melted onto the enormous amount of paperwork Cole's foster dad kept on his desk. From there, it had been a quick jump to the curtains, which had been homemade and not even close to fire retardant. The investigation determined that from the time the fire started until the house was completely engulfed had been less than twenty minutes.

Shaye swore again, louder this time, and Marcos's voice came through the door, "Shaye, is everything okay?"

"Yeah, sorry. Headache is actually feeling better. I'll be out soon."

There was a pause, then: "Whatever you're up to, just call me if you need help, okay?"

"Okay," she said weakly, embarrassed she was so transparent. She heard his footsteps moving away, and she stared down at her tablet.

Twenty minutes. Twenty minutes for eight people to run out of that house, where any pause or delay could have cost them their lives. And Cole had stopped twice, once for each of his brothers.

The sob caught her unexpectedly, and Shaye took a deep breath. She looked up at the ceiling and said a quick prayer of thanks that she'd gotten to meet Cole at all.

And maybe she'd misunderstood his tone when he'd told her about the report. Because the arson investigation looked solid from what she knew about those things. There were no signs that the fire had been intentionally set. Except...

Shaye frowned and clicked on a linked file, an addendum that had been added only a week ago. Then her breath caught again as she read through the new information.

Cole was right. The fire that had been set all those years ago *hadn't* been an accident.

Chapter Fifteen

"How did it go?" Shaye met Cole anxiously at the door as soon as he walked in. Marcos stood more slowly behind her.

She tried to hide her nerves from both of them, but the way she was wringing her hands was probably a dead giveaway that something was wrong. Marcos had definitely noticed when she'd come out from the guest bedroom an hour ago. But she'd wanted to talk to Cole about what she'd found first, then let him be the one to tell his brothers.

She tried to focus on what he'd expect her to want to know. After he and Luke had dropped her off here a few hours ago, they'd taken off again to talk to Ken Tobek.

The more she'd thought about it, the more strongly she felt about him as a possible suspect. When she'd given her testimony in court, he'd sat impassively, probably trying to appear innocent and apologetic. But when she'd passed him in the hallway afterward, the way he'd narrowed his eyes at her, almost snarling...it still gave her chills.

Cole sidestepped her, closing and locking the door behind him. Then he took her hand and pulled her toward the couch, earning a raised eyebrow from Marcos.

Shaye's pulse started a crescendo. She'd been trying not to dwell on that lustful look Cole had given her back at the station, but it had been hard not to, even while she'd been distracting herself looking up information on the fire. But that didn't mean she wanted a repeat in front of someone else.

So, for now, she focused on her case. She'd worry about giving Cole the bad news about the fire later. "What did Tobek say? Did you see the Taurus?"

Cole settled on the couch, keeping his hand tucked in hers as Marcos sat back on the chair, looking curious but keeping quiet. "He denied it, of course. He still blames everyone else for what he did, but there's no sign of the Taurus. And his alibi looks solid. We spoke to the coworker who alibied him, too, after we saw Tobek. That guy seems to be generally nervous, so it's hard to tell what spooked him or didn't, but I can't see any reason for him to lie for Tobek."

"Maybe he's being paid," Shaye suggested.

"We laid into him pretty good, trying to scare him about what would happen about lying during a police investigation, but he stuck to his story. And his and Tobek's were consistent. Plus this guy is young—about fifteen years younger than Tobek. Jumps at his own shadow. I think he would have broken if Tobek had paid him off."

Cole's thumb started absently stroking her hand. "We'll keep digging, talk to the brother-in-law about the Taurus, but we need to check into other suspects. I don't like Tobek, but I'm not sure he'd risk trying to gun someone down in public. Honestly, he strikes me as the kind of guy who hits his wife behind closed doors and then goes out and chats up his neighbors. Following a police car to get to you? I don't know."

"Do any of the other suspects look promising?" Marcos spoke up.

Shaye had almost forgotten he was there, the way Cole's thumb was sliding over the sensitive skin on the back of her hand. She'd almost forgotten *everything* she needed to be thinking about right now.

Cole's shoulders slumped. "Not really. But we've broadened the list, trying to look at anyone remotely connected to Shaye. This guy holds a personal grudge, which means he's connected to a case or connected to her. We'll find him."

"Let me know if I can help," Marcos said, standing up and stretching his arms. His gaze dropped to their linked hands. "I'm going to head home and let you two be alone."

"Thanks," Cole said, dropping her hand to give his brother a hug and walk him to the door.

Then he was sliding the lock and leaning against the closed door, the expression on his face pure hunger. And 100 percent directed at her.

Shaye's breathing went shallow as two years' worth of daydreams about Cole Walker suddenly seemed possible. She tried to shake it off, tried to focus. She had something important she needed to tell him, but the longer he looked at her, the more her mind seemed to go fuzzy and her body took over.

"Shaye," Cole said, his voice huskier than usual as he pushed away from the door and headed toward her.

There was no doubt about it. He was going to kiss her.

But had anything really changed? Last night he'd told her nothing could ever happen between them. So what was going on? Was this supposed to be a onetime thing? And if she had a fling with him, would she ever recover from the heartbreak? Could she even do anything without first coming clean about what she'd just discovered about his past?

He kept coming, slowly, purposefully, and she knew she had to make up her mind.

"Cole," she said, and her own voice didn't sound quite right, either. "I—"

He watched her carefully, waiting for whatever she was going to say.

And then she made up her mind.

COLE COULD SEE it the instant Shaye made a decision. If only he knew what choice she'd made. She was giving him mixed signals, still eyeing him like she wanted to swallow him whole, but with one hand up. Not that he could complain too much after the mixed signals he'd been giving her. Still, he hoped the whole eating-him-alive thing won out.

"I have to tell you something," Shaye said, her voice wobbly as she dropped her hand.

A satisfied smile threatened, because he knew why she was struggling to speak. But he held it in and asked, "Is it about us?"

Furrows appeared between her eyebrows. "Not exactly. It's about the past—"

"Unless it's about you and me and all the ways I'd like to show you how stupid I've been these past few days with my lips and my tongue, let's save it for later, okay?"

"Uh…" She gave a nervous laugh, and he took a step closer.

Cole let his gaze drop over her, from the top of those curls piled on her head, down over the simple blue blouse and black pants that hugged her in all the right places. He came back up just as slowly, lingering on the spots he was desperate to kiss, until he met her eyes.

She was staring back wide-eyed, desire and uncertainty battling.

He took another step; all he'd have to do was reach out his hand and he'd be touching her. But he resisted, waiting, hoping she'd give him the okay to do all the things he'd been dreaming about since the moment he'd first seen her. The longer he'd known her, those dreams had gotten more detailed and more intense.

"What happened?" she whispered, her voice suddenly scratchy. She licked her lips, and his eyes were glued to the movement.

"What do you mean?"

"Yesterday you said—"

"Yesterday I was being an idiot."

"You've changed your mind?" She reached out tentatively, let her hand glide over the buttons on his shirt, barely touching him, but sending desire zigzagging through his body.

He wanted to lie and say yes, because he sensed that one word was all it would take to get him to heaven. But he couldn't do that. "Depends what you mean."

She frowned. "I mean about you saying we were too different to make a relationship last."

"I still think that."

She dropped her hand away from his body.

"But I'm willing to try anyway."

"I don't understand." The desire in her gaze was starting to clear, replaced by confusion and wariness.

"I still think that long-term, our differences are going to get in the way." He took her hand, slid his fingers between hers. It was such a perfect fit. "But you were right, too, when you said we'd be good together. I think we would."

She pulled her hand free slowly. "Cole, I—I've never had a fling with anyone."

"That's—"

"Hear me out. I care about you a lot, and I know myself. As much as I may want you, I don't think I can go into a one-night—"

"That's not what I'm asking for," Cole cut her off, not wanting her to think for a second that he'd expect one night and nothing more. As if one taste of Shaye would be enough.

Would any amount of Shaye be enough? The thought made panic flutter briefly, but he pushed it down. "I'm in this for as long as you are. I promise you that."

She stared at him, and the seconds drew out as he tried to read her gaze. Then he didn't have to, because she launched herself into his arms.

COLE'S ARMS LOCKED around her waist. No sooner had she lifted up on her tiptoes than his mouth was crashing down on hers. He kissed her with desperation, like he'd been waiting to do it for years, nipping at her lips with his teeth, licking at them with his tongue, his soft beard rasping against her chin. The moment she sighed and opened her mouth, his tongue slipped inside, and Shaye's knees buckled.

He bent low, scooped one hand under her knees and lifted her. Then they were moving, and Shaye didn't care where, just as long as it was somewhere horizontal so she could feel his whole body pressed to hers and ease the ache inside her. He kept kissing her as they walked, frantic, passionate kisses that matched exactly the need she felt. Only it still wasn't enough.

Sliding her hands through his hair, she got distracted by the softness of it, the contrast to the slick feel of his tongue exploring her mouth so thoroughly and the hardness of his chest against her side. Then he was laying her down, and she opened her eyes, realizing she was in his bedroom.

She gave herself a brief moment to glance around, curious, since she'd been too distracted by worry last time she'd been in here. She took in the framed family pictures on his dresser, the clothes stacked on a chair in the corner like he hadn't had time to put them away. The walls were a light blue, almost the color of Cole's eyes, and she looked back at him.

He was still standing beside the bed, a soft smile on his face unlike any smile she'd ever seen from him. There was desire in it, but something more, something tender.

And suddenly she knew what his words had meant.

She was in love with him, but yesterday she'd tried to convince herself she was strong enough to move on. And she would have been; she'd proven it to herself when she'd been about to turn down his offer, thinking it was for one night. His words in the living room had confused her at first. How could he be completely committed to a relationship if he was still sure they were too different to last? But now she understood. He'd said he was in it as long as she was—he was just certain *she'd* eventually get tired of *him.*

He hadn't rejected her yesterday because he'd been uninterested in a relationship with her; he'd rejected her because he'd been scared of one.

But right now, with him staring at her with that softness in his eyes, like he'd do anything for her, she realized something else. He loved her, too. He probably didn't even know it yet, but he did. She was suddenly certain of that fact.

Her heart started beating even faster, and then he was climbing onto the bed with her, carefully lowering himself on top of her. Her body arched up to meet him, and a low moan escaped at the first feel of him against her, at the sheer giddiness of knowing how deeply he cared for her.

He groaned in response. "Shaye," he whispered. "You're killing my self-control here."

The idea that she could have that effect on him made her feel powerful and intensely happy. She wiggled her hips a little, giving him a devious grin.

He smiled back at her, laughter in the quirk of his lips. Then his fingers were threading with hers, lifting them up over her head. She expected his mouth to dive back to hers, and she craned her neck, reaching for him, but he didn't meet her. Instead he bent his head to her neck, then her ear, making her squirm.

She tugged her hands free, needing to feel him, and then his hands were buried in her hair, yanking out the bun. He combed through it with his fingers, spreading her hair over the pillow behind her, all the while doing things to her earlobe with his tongue that made spots form in front of her eyes.

Sliding her hands down over his back, she tried to get underneath his button-down, to better feel all the muscles that had rippled under her touch. She couldn't quite reach, so she grabbed a handful of his shirt and tugged it upward.

Cole swore, then moved her hands and stood up. "Sorry, honey. You're making it hard to think straight." He unhooked the holster from his belt and stuck it in his bedside table, then he was getting back into bed, but this time he pulled her on top of him.

"Oh." Shaye twined her legs with his, liking the feel of him underneath her. She scooted up on her elbows, so she could undo the buttons on his shirt, and he used the opportunity to tackle hers. Before she had his half unbuttoned, he was sliding the sleeves down her arms, yanking them away from him. "Hey!"

"Mmm," Cole murmured, his gaze locked on the blue silk bra she was suddenly very happy she'd decided to put on this morning.

Then his hands were sliding around her waist, and she found herself being pulled upward. Shaye caught herself on the pillow, laughing. "What are you…" She trailed off on a moan as his tongue slid under the edge of her bra.

"You taste good," he mumbled against her skin, and her whole body seemed to heat up another couple of degrees.

Hooking her thighs around him, she pulled herself back downward, fusing her mouth to his, desperate for the feel of his lips against hers again. Then she was up on her knees, with him sitting under her. She rocked against him, fumbling to get her hands between them again to finish his buttons. Finally she had them undone, and she could slide her palms up and down his chest and abs.

Muscles contracted under her every touch,

and then he was tugging her knees, pulling her tighter against him until she tipped her head back and moaned. His lips returned to her neck, then worked their way downward again. She felt cool air on the back of her thighs and realized he'd managed to undo the hooks on her pants and slip them down to her knees.

She could barely breathe as he slid one of her bra straps down, trailing his hand with his mouth, while the other hand cupped her butt, the imprint of him hot through her silk panties. She sank down on his lap and then his mouth was on hers again, the pace of his kisses increasing as his hands slid up and down her body. His hands moved slowly, like he was learning every inch of her—or just trying to drive her even crazier.

She was going to make love to Cole Walker. And wow, was the reality turning out to be even better than any of the thousands of fantasies she'd had about him over the past two years.

"Shaye," he breathed, like he was right in tune with her, feeling the same thing.

Then his phone rang, making her jump as it vibrated against her butt. He tugged her back down, ignoring it, his fingers slipping under the waistband of her panties as she reached for his belt.

It stopped ringing, then started up again almost immediately. Cole swore, lifted her off him like she weighed nothing and dug in his pocket, struggling to yank out his phone. "What?" he snapped as he answered it.

The volume must have been turned up high, because Luke's voice came through clearly as he laughed. "Uh, sorry. Am I interrupting something? Because I've got a lot of news."

"Yes, you're interrupting something," Cole said tightly. "Is this a lot of news I have to hear right this second?"

"Yeah, I'm afraid so."

The desire slipped off Cole's face, replaced by what Shaye had come to think of as his detective expression. "What is it?"

"Well, first, Elliard escaped custody at the hospital."

"What?" Cole swiped his hand across his forehead, glancing at her. His gaze wandered downward and she realized the desire was still there; it was just hidden. "Do we have people looking for him?"

"Yeah, but there's more, and this is the main reason I called. Remember that anonymous tip we got the other day about a gun in the water near the Kings' territory?"

"What about it?"

"They ran it at the lab. Cole, it's the gun that was used to shoot at Shaye."

Chapter Sixteen

"Can we just hit Pause on this?" Cole asked, his eyes glued to her. "Maybe you could wait here, just like this, until I get back?"

Shaye was leaning up against his headboard, her hair loose around her shoulders and a mess from his fingers. Her shirt was gone, somewhere on his floor, and one of her bra straps dangled down her shoulder. She'd tugged her pants back up but hadn't bothered to button them, and he could still see a hint of the underwear he'd been about to slide down when Luke had called.

A thousand swearwords lodged in his throat

at the idea of leaving, but this was big news. The gun being found in Kings territory meant that Leonardo was probably lying. Either he *had* okayed Elliard going after Shaye, or he'd okayed the rest of his gang helping Elliard get revenge on the station. On him.

All of *that* meant that Cole wanted every last Kings member rounded up and at the station immediately.

"How long do you plan to be gone?" Shaye asked, her voice suggestive, like she was actually considering waiting in his bed for him in her underwear until he returned.

Cole's body reacted immediately, and he seriously considered calling Luke back and saying he'd be at the station in an hour. But half an hour with Shaye wasn't going to be nearly good enough, and especially not the first time. "I wish I was serious about you waiting right here," he said. "But this will probably take all night."

Her shoulders slumped, and he climbed into bed, crawling toward her, then planting a long kiss on her lips. "But this is almost over now. We have the gun. We're going to bring everyone in and keep them there until someone talks." He lifted her hand to his lips, pressed a kiss to her palm. "And then I'm going to lock the door, turn off the phone and stay in bed with you for an entire day. What do you think?"

"I like it," she replied, a little breathless. "Now hurry."

Cole laughed. "Yes, ma'am." He got out of bed, already missing her, and redid his belt. Forgoing the shirt she'd tossed on the floor, he grabbed a clean one and buttoned it up, then looked at his watch and frowned. "I'm going to see which of my brothers can head back over here."

"Just go," Shaye said. "Leave your poor brothers alone. This guy doesn't know where you live, or he would have already been here."

"Yeah, well, Elliard is on the run, so I'm not taking any chances."

"If Elliard was the shooter, he couldn't even figure out where *I* live, and my personal information is easier to find than yours," Shaye said.

It wouldn't surprise him if she had looked, given her computer skills.

"Well, I'm calling them anyway," Cole said, grabbing his cell and trying Andre first. When Andre picked up, he told Cole he'd just been called out for a mission. "Stay safe," Cole told him, then called Marcos.

"Sorry to ask you to turn right back around," Cole said.

"No problem," Marcos replied, sounding tired. "Be there in twenty."

Cole hung up, then sat back down on the bed with Shaye. "How do you feel about some good old-fashioned necking while we wait for Marcos?" he teased her, wiggling his eyebrows.

But Shaye looked serious all of a sudden.

"Don't worry. I'll be careful, and we're close. I can feel it," he told her.

"It's not that," Shaye said, scooting closer and taking his hand. "I need to tell you something."

"What?" Nerves overtook him. What had she said before? "Something about the past?"

"Yeah. I know I didn't ask you first, and I hope you're not going to be upset, but I looked up information about the fire."

A jolt went through him. Shaye had always been able to pull things from digital devices, from the vastness of the internet, that no one else he knew could find.

His throat went dry. "What did you discover?"

She squeezed his hand. "It wasn't an accident."

"Are you sure? How do you know?" Before she could answer, he sighed and dropped his head. "It was Andre who brought it up, during his girlfriend's case you helped us with. He had this dream and—" Cole broke off, swearing. "He remembered that our foster dad and one of the foster kids came from the back office, where the fire started. It was the middle of the night—well, nearing dawn, I guess, but it felt like the middle of the night. Everyone should have been upstairs asleep."

"But they weren't," Shaye said, and he wasn't sure if it was a statement or a question.

"No. It actually wasn't the fire that woke me exactly. It was the noise. My foster mom yelling, then I saw her run past my room, out of her bedroom at the end of the hall. And then the other two foster brothers we lived with—I can't even remember their names anymore, but I shared a room with them. They were falling out of bed and running. And I got up and..."

He let out a heavy breath as the memories overtook him, the sheer panic, the unbearable heat, the smoke that made it hard to breathe. Then desperation to get to Andre and Marcos in the bedroom down the hall.

"You did it," Shaye said softly, somehow even closer than she'd been before, although he hadn't felt her move. "You got them out."

"Sort of," he said. "We lost Marcos on the way down the stairs. I thought he was behind us still, but—"

"But he made it," she reminded him, stroking his arm. "They're both okay."

"Yeah." His jaw tightened. "But it could have turned out different. Who set the fire? My foster dad?"

"No." Shaye shook her head. "Another foster kid. Brenna Hartwell. There was a juvenile record attached to the old arson report that had just been unsealed this week. It says she set it for kicks, and it got out of hand."

Cole frowned, angry and sad at the same time. "Brenna was eleven. We considered that she set it, that maybe something bad was happening with our foster dad we didn't know about, since they were back there together, but she did it for fun?" He sighed heavily as the doorbell rang. "Marcos isn't going to take this well. She was his first crush."

"I'm sorry," Shaye said.

He kissed her forehead. "Thanks for caring about me enough to look into this. I don't like the answers, but at least I know."

Then he stood. "Now I'm going to go and get some answers for you."

SHAYE PACED BACK and forth in Cole's bedroom. She'd been unable to sit still waiting with Marcos in the living room, but she hadn't wanted to show him just how nervous she was. She'd claimed exhaustion and headed for the bedroom.

She'd debated a minute in the hallway whether to return to the guest room or just wait in Cole's, and she'd finally decided on his room. He'd suggested she stay here anyway, and even though he'd been half joking, she knew he wouldn't mind. Besides, this way Marcos would have somewhere to sleep besides the couch if Cole was at the station late. Which she suspected he would be, since he was literally bringing in an entire gang.

She couldn't believe she was back here again, with a gang threat over her head. *Another day, another gang.* She let out a choked laugh at the thought, but the reality was the fear she'd been trying so hard to battle was returning with a vengeance.

It was like a year ago in replay: she was hiding again while Cole was out there putting himself in danger, trying to keep her safe. She prayed he could pull off the same miracle twice.

"You okay in there, Shaye?" Marcos's voice came through the door.

"Yeah, sorry. I'm a little stressed out. I'm going to go to bed."

"Don't worry," Marcos said. "Do what you need to do. If you need company, I'm here, okay?"

"Thanks." The word came out garbled as she choked up a little. Cole's brothers had treated her like family since the moment Cole had first introduced her to them.

His footsteps echoed as he walked back to the living room and Shaye locked the door just so he wouldn't come back and check on her while she was changing. She stripped out of her clothes, grabbed a T-shirt off the pile on Cole's chair and slipped it over her head, breathing in the scent of his laundry detergent.

Then she crawled into his bed and closed her eyes, hoping when she opened them again, he'd be climbing in beside her.

The *creak* pulled her partway out of sleep, and she rolled over, still groggy, her hand reaching for the other side of the bed. But it was cold and empty.

Sleep pulled at her again, a dream where Cole was home and safe and all the threats facing him in his job every day no longer existed. But why did he smell like he'd been drinking? Shaye sniffed and frowned.

Then there was another *creak*, and she realized it was coming from the wrong direction to be Marcos.

She opened her eyes, shooting up in bed, her hand reaching out instinctively for something to grab as a weapon, searching for a lamp on the bedside table. She struck a mug, and it slipped off, hitting the floor and shattering.

She blinked in the darkness, thinking she'd been imagining a threat, when she was yanked out of bed and a hand clamped down over her mouth. The scent of liquor seemed to surround her, acrid in her nostrils.

Shaye flailed, kicking, trying to elbow her

assailant as she heard Marcos's footsteps pounding toward the room.

Then something cold and sharp pressed against her neck, and a deep voice whispered in her ear. "Make him walk away or I slice you open right here."

Going completely still was her only option as she identified the object at her throat. A knife. A very big, very sharp knife. Every breath made it push into her skin, threatening to break through.

"Shaye! You okay?" Marcos called.

"Do it," the voice whispered, sending shivers down her arms.

"I'm fine," Shaye called, but her voice came out weak and shaky, because with each word she could feel the knife's edge more.

The man behind her—someone not much taller than her but with a lot more strength than his size suggested—moved the knife to give her a little space.

The doorknob started to turn, then caught because she'd locked it.

"He leaves or you're not the only one to die," the man growled in her ear, his mouth moving against her skin in a way that was making her desperate to squirm away from him.

His arm shifted alongside her. When she looked down, she saw a pistol in his gloved hand, pointing at the door.

The handle stopped moving, and Shaye knew what was coming next. Marcos would kick it down. And Marcos would die.

She'd always been a bad liar. Shaye closed her eyes and risked precious seconds taking a calming breath. "Sorry about that," she called out, her voice clear and calm. "I had a bad dream and knocked over Cole's coffee mug."

There was a pause. "Why's the door locked?"

"I, um—" She tried to sound embarrassed. "I got hot and went to bed in my underwear."

There was low laughter in the hallway, and

relief slumped Shaye's shoulders. "You're going to make my brother really happy. He's on his way back."

"In case I'm asleep when he gets in," Shaye said quickly as the knife pressed hard against her neck again, "tell him…"

She paused so long that Marcos just said softly, "He knows, Shaye."

"Tell him I was right," she rushed on quickly, as the voice in her ear suddenly clicked into place and she thought she recognized it. *Maybe.*

"Right about what?" Marcos asked, a hint of concern creeping back in.

"His bed is more comfortable than mine," she said, and the knife eased up again.

There was more soft laughter from the hall. "I'll let him know. Good night, Shaye."

"Good night."

The footsteps headed away again. The voice whispered in her ear. "Good job. Now keep following directions, and I won't have to kill him *or* your boyfriend."

He spun her around and she realized what the noises she'd heard earlier were: he'd cut a hole in the window and then opened it, climbing inside that way. Now he pushed her toward it, in her bare feet and Cole's T-shirt. "You're going first. And remember—I have a gun. So I wouldn't try making a run for it."

Shaye swallowed hard, her gaze darting to the closed door, the scent of alcohol—was it whiskey?—so strong it was making her gag. But she still couldn't make out the face of her abductor, only pray that she was right about his voice sounding familiar. Because otherwise, if Marcos and Cole managed to decipher her clue, she'd be sending them in the wrong direction.

The knife jabbed her in the back, pricking through the T-shirt and into her skin. She muffled a yelp, then climbed carefully out the window.

He was outside behind her before she could even consider making a run for it, and then he was shoving her along to a sedan parked at the curb. He popped the trunk. "Get in."

She started to turn toward him, and that knife jabbed her again, sending tears to her eyes. There was no question: if she climbed into this trunk right now, she was going to die.

She hesitated briefly, then climbed inside.

Chapter Seventeen

"How'd it go?" Marcos greeted Cole when he came home.

Cole sighed, kicking off his shoes and sinking onto the couch beside his brother. "Not great. We rounded up the whole gang and put them all into holding or interrogation rooms. Luke and I leaned on them pretty hard, but they're more scared of Leonardo than us."

"That's not surprising," Marcos said. "That guy has a reputation."

"Yeah, I know, but I was hoping that someone would be scared enough of *us* after what we did to their competition to talk. Honestly, I thought we had a shot with Leonardo himself handing over the shooter."

"Where are they now?" Marcos asked. "You have to let them all go?"

Cole gave a halfhearted grin. "Nope. We figured out a way to hang on to them all for now. We'll see if a night in jail makes them realize we're not giving up until the Kings go the way of the Jannis Crew if they don't give us some answers."

"Your girl has been in bed for a while."

"Good. I figured as much when she didn't greet me at the door. She's a worrier."

"It can't be easy, dating someone in law enforcement," Marcos said.

"Yeah, I guess not." It was something he'd worried about from the start with Shaye; it wasn't fair to drag her into that kind of life. Cole rested his head on the back of the couch, still anxious to go join Shaye, but wanting to decompress a little first. He knew she'd wake up and he'd need to reassure her he was fine.

"Especially after what she went through last year."

Cole lifted his head, looking at his brother. "Did she say something to you?"

"No. But she was a ball of nerves all evening. She finally went and hid in your room so she could pace in there without me seeing."

A small smile lifted the corners of his lips. "That sounds like Shaye."

"By the way, she told me to tell you she was right about your bed being more comfortable than hers."

"What?" Cole shook his head, perplexed. Had she ever said something like that? He didn't think so, but then he'd been so focused on getting his lips and hands on her, maybe he'd missed it.

"I should go," Marcos said, standing. "Let you go reassure her you're okay."

"You're welcome to stay," Cole said. "Save the drive for the morning."

"Nah. I'll let you two have some privacy. A word of advice though, big brother? Hang on to that one. For a computer nerd, she's pretty special." He grinned.

Cole swore.

"I'm just kidding about the computer nerd thing."

"No, it's not that. Sit down for a second, would you?"

Marcos sat, looking wary. "Why? What's going on?"

Cole shifted to face his brother, knowing he needed to tell Marcos now, instead of delaying things. "Shaye did some digging into our past."

There was a long pause, and then Marcos tensed and shook his head, surely realizing why Cole looked so grim right now. They'd talked about the possibility that Brenna was involved when Andre had first realized the fire might not be accidental. "I don't believe it."

"There was an unsealed juvie record, Marcos. She admitted she did it."

"She must have had a reason. Maybe—"

"She said she did it for fun, and things got out of hand."

"Then why was our foster father down there? No, I don't buy it."

"He probably heard something and caught her doing it," Cole said. "I'm sorry. I know you had a crush on her when we were kids."

"She was so alone. So sad," Marcos said, looking sad himself. "I can't believe—"

"I'm sorry," Cole repeated. "I just wanted you to know."

"Have you told Andre yet?"

"No, but I'll give him a call tomorrow."

Marcos clapped a hand on his shoulder and stood again. "You have enough on your plate. I can do it."

"That's not—"

"It's fine," Marcos said, but his usual noth-ing-gets-me-down expression was gone, look-ing like someone had given it a solid kick. "Say good-night to Shaye for me."

Cole walked him to the door, his heart heavy as he closed it behind Marcos. Then he headed for the bedroom, anxious to curl up beside Shaye and get a little sleep.

NEVER LET ANYONE lock you in the trunk.

Shaye was pretty sure that was safety rule number one. When she'd gotten inside, she hadn't seen any other options. There was no-where to run that her abductor wouldn't be able to shoot her. And then Marcos would run out-side, and what if he got shot, too?

If it had been just her, she might have risked it over whatever this guy had planned for her whenever they got where they were going. But she couldn't risk Cole's brother.

But now she wished she'd tried *something*. What exactly she could have tried, she still wasn't sure.

The car bounced over something at a speed high enough she knew they must have been on a freeway. Shaye bounced with it, her head banging against the trunk even as she tried to brace herself. Then she rolled, slamming into one side and then the other. Tears stung her eyes, but at least there was nothing else in the trunk to hit. Of course, if there had been, maybe she could have armed herself for when the vehicle eventually stopped.

Even thinking about what might be coming made her panic, and she started to hyperventilate. Shaye closed her eyes, bracing her feet and hands on either end of the trunk as she focused on taking deep breaths. It was awkward and hard to get a good angle the way she was folded in here, but the next time he ran over something—what the heck was on this freeway?—she didn't move as much.

Her hands and feet started to ache, and the places he'd pricked her with the knife stung. It was pitch-black, so she had no idea how badly she was hurt. Before he'd gotten moving so fast, she'd probed at the wounds, trying to find out. She was definitely bleeding, but as much as they hurt, she didn't think it was bad. It wouldn't be those injuries that would kill her.

Calm down, Shaye reminded herself, trying to think. She had no weapons. No idea where she was going. And she was in bare feet and Cole's T-shirt, which kept riding up past her underwear as she was tossed around the trunk. A thousand new worst-case scenarios ran through her mind.

Kick out the taillights.

The idea flashed through her mind out of nowhere, and she remembered a case she'd read about in graduate school where a girl who'd been kidnapped had done that. She'd still been killed by her captor, but her DNA on the broken taillight he'd later had fixed had landed him in jail.

Shaye shifted, trying to reposition herself as she searched for the taillights. But all she felt was carpeting. Except…

She pried at a seam with her fingernails and it peeled away. Part of one fingernail broke off and the forensic specialist in her thought about how, as long as he didn't vacuum too carefully, that piece of her could convict him if she wasn't around to do it.

Stop it, Shaye silently yelled at herself, but it was hard not to think about her death. She didn't know why he hadn't simply killed her at Cole's house—except maybe that would make it too difficult to get away. But she had no doubt that was his intention.

"The taillight," Shaye muttered. She was so panicked, she wasn't thinking right. She felt around behind the cover she'd broken off and there it was: the back of the taillight! Excitement filled her and Shaye tried to shove the light out with her hands, but it didn't budge.

She blinked back the tears that filled her eyes, then scooted around again until her feet were positioned over the taillight. Knowing it was going to be painful with her bare feet, she closed her eyes, braced herself and then kicked with all her might.

The taillight snapped free, shooting out of the car, and Shaye's right foot slammed the metal edge while her left one went partially through it, bending her toes at an impossible angle. She screamed at the pain that raced up her leg, but didn't waste any time before spinning around again.

Ignoring the throbbing, she put her eye up to the hole. If she could stick her hand out and wave, maybe another car on the freeway would see her and call the police.

But when she peered outside, all she saw was darkness, and she realized that she'd been so focused on her plan she hadn't noticed the car slowing. They were no longer on the freeway.

The car made a turn, then came to a stop and the engine turned off.

Shaye made one last desperate search for a weapon, her hands tracing over the whole trunk. They grasped the cover of the taillight. It was pathetic and flimsy, but it was all she had.

Holding in tears, she gripped it in both hands as the trunk slowly opened.

Chapter Eighteen

"Shaye?" Cole tried not to panic. She'd undoubtedly been exhausted, so maybe she'd fallen into an especially heavy sleep.

But he'd been knocking on the door for more than a minute, and he was practically yelling her name now. He took a deep breath and hoped she'd forgive him, then stepped back and leveled a hard kick at the door, right beside the doorknob, like he'd do if he had to break down a door at a suspect's house.

It splintered, and a quick jab with his shoulder pushed it the rest of the way in. It hung off the frame, revealing an empty room.

Shaye was gone.

Now the panic had free rein as he took in his bedroom. His covers were rumpled, the comforter half on the floor. There was a broken mug beside his bed. Had there been a struggle? But if so, why hadn't his brother heard anything?

His blood pressure rising by the second, Cole grabbed his cell phone and texted Marcos a quick message: Get back here now.

Then he went to the window, noticing the glass on the ground, along with a little bit of blood. The window was closed, and there was a neat circle cut into the glass, made by the type of tool a professional would have.

Cole unholstered his weapon and ran to the front door. He whipped it open and was just clearing his porch when Marcos's car screeched to a stop at his curb. Then his brother was running toward him.

"What is it?" Marcos asked, drawing his own weapon.

"Shaye is gone."

"What?" Marcos shook his head. "I talked to her less than an hour ago. She was in your room. She sounded..."

"What?" Cole spun to face his brother.

"She sounded odd at first. I almost broke down the door, and then she said everything was fine. We had a conversation through the door." He swore. "You think someone was in there with her?"

"I don't know." Cole checked the immediate area for any unfamiliar cars. "Follow me. Let's check the back. She went out the window. Someone definitely came in from outside. If we don't see anything there, we get Luke and the rest of my department down here."

"I've got your back," Marcos said as the two of them rounded the corner of the house, making their way quickly to the window outside Cole's bedroom.

Cole used his phone to shine a light at the ground. "More glass, but just a little." He shook his head as he glanced around. His house backed up to his neighbors' yards. An unlikely route for a kidnapper. "He must have had a car waiting. She could be anywhere by now."

"I'm so sorry," Marcos said. "I can't believe I didn't—"

"It's not your fault," Cole said, and he meant it. His brother was good at his job, and if he hadn't realized someone had come into the house, the guy must have been silent and quick. And it wasn't as if Cole had told Marcos not to take his eyes off her. Cole had thought she'd be safe in his house. Having his brother there had just been a precaution.

Marcos was fiddling with his phone, and a second later, he had it to his ear. "Luke? It's

Marcos. Shaye is missing. We need your help." There was a pause, then Marcos said, "Yeah, bring the cavalry."

"We have to find her," Cole said. His voice sounded broken and scared. He should have realized this threat was too big as soon as the gangs got involved again. He should have disregarded his own selfish need to keep her in his life and insisted she go into Witness Protection. Better he never see her again, if it meant she'd have been safe.

What if he never saw her again?

Marcos's words broke through his frenzied thoughts. "We'll find her."

"How? This guy could have taken her anywhere by now." He couldn't bring himself to say the words out loud, but he also couldn't turn his law enforcement brain off. Because years as a cop had taught him the awful reality: Shaye could already be dead by now.

"LISTEN UP," LUKE SAID, sounding like a drill instructor as his voice cut through the noise, quieting the cluster of cops in Cole's living room.

Cole knocked the handful of items off his coffee table and spread a map there. "Shaye disappeared within the last hour and a half out of this house." If her abductor had gotten on the freeway, she could be quite a distance away by now. Heck, she could be in another state. But most perpetrators stuck to what they knew, because it was easier to control the variables. Which meant places the police could track— Cole hoped.

"We still have all the Kings members locked up," Hiroshi said. "And we have a pretty good handle on that group, right? Could there be someone in the gang we don't know about? Someone who could pull this off?"

"Unlikely, but we're not taking any chances.

We've got Dawson and Pietrich back at the station laying into the gangsters again," Luke said.

And there were a pair of lab techs in Cole's bedroom, searching for prints, though Cole figured that was unlikely to yield anything. Someone who'd managed to stay one step ahead of them for this long would have worn gloves to break into a police detective's house.

"Meanwhile, our best bet is that Elliard took her," Cole said. "He's still not accounted for, and the timing fits."

"He was in pretty bad shape still, wasn't he?" one of the officers asked. "I mean, the hospital wasn't even ready to discharge him when he snuck out. Would he have the strength to abduct someone?"

"He escaped custody at the hospital," Luke reminded them. "Which means he managed to get out of the cuffs tethering him to the bed and past his guard and then out of the hospital without being spotted. So, he must have been in better shape than he was letting on. Plus, we're assuming he's managed to acquire a weapon since then, and if that's the case, he wouldn't really need to rely on muscle when he took Shaye, just firepower."

"But we're not ruling out anyone," Cole added. He pointed at two officers in the corner. "I want you two to pay Ken Tobek a visit. His alibi seems pretty solid for the shooting, but apparently his brother-in-law owns an old Taurus. Make Tobek call the brother-in-law. Get the location of that Taurus."

"Cole and I are going to run down Elliard's haunts," Luke said.

"I thought he didn't own anything," Hiroshi spoke up.

"He doesn't. We've got his sisters' houses and we've got known Kings hideouts to check, so we'll take some help covering those," Cole said, trying to sound confident. But inside the dread he'd been feeling since he'd broken down his bedroom door just kept growing. Elliard probably *did* have somewhere that was his own, even if his name didn't appear on any papers they could find. It was why he and Luke were going to talk to Rosa, because she was the person most likely to know where that was.

"We also want a pair of you to start making phone calls to everyone at the lab. See if any of them noticed someone watching Shaye. They might have a different perspective on it than she did. If you get anything, call us right away," Luke said.

Cole prayed they'd get something from that; it was actually one of his strongest hopes for new information if Elliard wasn't behind this, because when Shaye got to work, she got so focused. She could have missed someone at the lab who had an unnatural fixation on her, but he bet her coworkers wouldn't. And someone at the lab would have a much easier time identifying where Shaye had been tonight than Elliard or another gang member.

"Meanwhile, all the officers out on patrol right now are watching for a car that fits the description of the one used during Shaye's shooting," Cole added, shaking off his contemplation. "If one is spotted, they'll tail it and call for backup. Don't approach this guy alone. Whoever he is, expect him to be armed and dangerous."

Cole looked around the room, thankful that all these officers were willing to drop everything and come here. He hadn't even questioned that they would, but it was touching. The brotherhood in blue ran deep.

He nodded at Marcos, who'd been standing silently in the corner the whole time. He knew Marcos still blamed himself, no matter what Cole had said, and he wasn't going to feel better until Shaye was back home and safe.

Cole's train of thought stuttered on the idea

that when he imagined Shaye home safe, it wasn't her home, it was *his*. His throat tightened. When had he gone from an infatuation with this woman to being in love with her? Had it been a slow development, happening a little at a time so he never even noticed? Or had he been fooling himself from the start, thinking he could ever just be friends with her or have something short-term?

Realizing Luke was staring at him expectantly, Cole cleared his throat and said, "Marcos is going to be staying here, coordinating everything. If you need anything, if you hear anything, call him. He'll get the word out."

Marcos would also be here in case Shaye managed to escape; meanwhile, he'd talk to Cole's neighbors to find out if any of them had heard or seen anything.

"Any questions?" Luke asked.

There was silence, until Hiroshi spoke up.

"We're going to find her. We won't stop until we do."

Cole nodded his thanks, praying they'd find her alive. "Let's do this. Let's find Shaye."

SHAYE READIED HER pathetic weapon, her heart thundering against her chest so hard it actually hurt. She tried to position her legs so she could pop up as soon as the trunk opened a little farther, but she was stiff and there wasn't a lot of space to get leverage.

Then it was happening. The trunk jolted open the rest of the way.

Before she could move, a bright light shone into her eyes and she instinctively shut them. The taillight cover was slapped out of her hands and she was wrenched out of the trunk, hard enough to send pain through her shoulders, like he'd pulled them out of their sockets. Her bare legs scraped the edge of the trunk and then she was on the cold ground, her T-shirt up around her waist.

She frantically yanked it down, simultaneously trying to get to her feet, when her captor warned her, "Get up slowly. I've still got a gun, and while it isn't my plan to shoot you right now, if you make me, I'll do it." A nasty edge suddenly came into his voice as he added, "Though I might just shoot you in the kneecaps to start. Not kill you straight out, but let you die slowly for wrecking my plan."

Shaye shivered. She tried not to, but she knew he'd seen it. If he wasn't planning to shoot her, what was his plan?

He had the flashlight aimed at her face again, so he just looked like a big man-shaped blur, but that voice was familiar. Was she right? And if she was, had Marcos even told Cole what she'd said? Had Cole understood? It hadn't been much of a hint, but she'd had to think fast, while trying not to let on anything was wrong to Marcos or let on to her abductor that she was trying to give away his identity.

The flashlight darted right. "Get up. Start walking."

She squinted, trying to see around the spots in front of her eyes to study his face, but the flashlight moved back to her too quickly. Why didn't he want her to see him? A tiny glimmer of hope surfaced. Could it be because he planned to let her live?

But if so, then what did he intend to do to her? Or was she simply bait, a way to lure Cole to him?

She needed to figure out an escape plan. Because from the little she could see, wherever she was right now was rural. As in, nowhere to run for help. And no one to hear her scream. And for someone who'd had enough liquor that it was practically seeping from his pores, her captor didn't seem to have lost any of his coordination or strength.

"Get up!"

Shaye scrambled, pushing to her feet and biting down on her tongue to keep from screaming at the pain that jolted through her shoulders. When she took a step, her left leg almost gave out on her, and she realized she'd broken some toes kicking out that taillight. And all for nothing.

"Go." The flashlight shifted again, aiming off to her right, and this time, instead of trying to see her captor, she followed it. Down a dirt trail was a dilapidated old barn, with red paint peeling and a roof that looked like it could collapse at any minute. If the barn was part of property that also had a house, she didn't see it.

How was anyone going to find her here?

Shoving down the panic, Shaye limped toward the barn, and her abductor followed, close enough that if she slowed down at all, he'd walk right into her. She went a little faster, holding down the edges of her T-shirt. Pebbles dug into her bare feet, and the spots he'd nicked her with the knife were throbbing.

"What is this about?" Shaye asked, hoping he'd tell her what he had planned for her. Maybe that way she'd know what she should do.

"What is this about?" he snapped, grabbing her arm and spinning her around. "You ruined my life and you don't even remember doing it?"

The more he spoke, the louder he was screaming, that whiskey scent shooting at her face, and still holding that flashlight on her, like he didn't want her to see him.

Why didn't he want her to see him?

"I don't… I can't—" Shaye stammered.

"Get in there." He shoved her forward.

She went down, landing on her knees. Shaye tried to get back up, but he put a boot in her side.

She yelped, clutching the spot as he reached past her and pulled open the door.

"Crawl," he growled at her.

Blinking back tears, she did, as pebbles scraped the cut on her leg. She made it just inside the doorway, before shock made her pause.

Tied up inside the barn was Dominic Elliard.

Chapter Nineteen

"Where is Dominic?" Cole demanded, jamming his shoulder against the door when Rosa's older sister tried to slam it in his face.

"I don't know!" she yelled at him, still struggling to push the door closed. "I haven't talked to him in years."

"But Rosa has," Luke said from slightly behind him on the stoop in the middle-class neighborhood out in the suburbs where Rosa's older sister lived.

"You can't do this," the woman grunted, leaning into the door harder. "This is my house."

"Your brother shot at a police station, then

escaped custody and kidnapped a forensic lab employee," Cole replied, tensing his shoulder muscles. This woman was tiny but strong.

At his words, she slumped and let go of the door so suddenly, he almost fell inside. "Come in," she told them. Then she yelled up the stairs, "Rosa! Get down here! Now!"

Cole kept his hand close to his side, unsnapping his holster in case he needed to make a quick grab for his weapon. He doubted Dominic was in the house, but he didn't want to find out he was wrong the hard way.

Luke followed behind him, and Cole knew he was keeping an eye on their surroundings as they followed Rosa and Dominic's sister into a brightly colored kitchen with sparkling appliances and kids' pictures on the refrigerator.

"You're lucky my husband took the kids to visit his parents this week," she said. Then she muttered, "I should have gone with them."

She gestured to the chairs at the kitchen table, but Cole shook his head. "We're in a hurry. We'd like to stop your brother from killing anyone today."

Her shoulders slumped and she sank into one of the chairs herself. "I thought he was finally going to get out of that life. Rosa said—"

"I said what?" Rosa asked, appearing in the doorway, scowling in a bathrobe, her hair hastily tied up on her head. She noticed Cole and Luke, and her lips turned up in a snarl. "Thanks for waking up the baby."

Cole tilted his head and realized that off in the distance, he could hear crying from upstairs. "We're sorry. We're in a rush. Your brother has kidnapped someone, and we don't have long before he kills her."

Rosa jerked, then shook her head. "No way."

"Have you seen him since he escaped custody, Rosa?" Luke asked softly.

"No." She shook her head. "No."

"Don't lie to us. You want your sister raising that baby because you're in jail as an accomplice?" Cole snapped, tired of messing around. Every second they wasted was more time for Dominic to kill Shaye.

He tried to push the thought from his mind, to focus the way he did for any other case, because if he couldn't, he knew he was useless to Shaye. But the thought of waking up tomorrow knowing that Shaye was gone for good, of going through the rest of his life without her, made his chest tighten until breathing hurt.

"What's wrong with him?"

The words seemed to come from a distance, then Luke's voice, closer, saying, "Nothing."

Then Luke was pushing him into a chair, pushing his head down, telling him to breathe.

Cole got a hold of himself, got the air back into his lungs. "Sorry, man."

"What just happened?" Rosa asked, sounding confused and afraid.

"It's his girlfriend your brother kidnapped. And he's not kidding when he says Dominic will kill her. He's already tried once, right before he came after Cole here at the police station." Rosa started to interrupt, and Luke said, "A whole station full of cops came when the call went out. We all saw him, Rosa."

"It's that stupid car." She sighed as her older sister glared at her, giving Rosa a silent "tell them everything" look.

"The car?" Luke pressed.

"Yeah, the car. He went crazy when you showed up that day. I honestly didn't think he'd go after you like that, but…he was so mad about what happened after Ed went away. I had nothing, me and the baby. I got canned from my job, because the manager found out I was Ed's girl, and he said he didn't want anything to do with the gangs. Then the pregnancy got rough, and I had to go on bed rest and I didn't know what to do. Dominic tried to help me, but he blamed the cops for taking everything Ed had, everything that should have been mine. When you came back for that car, it was the last straw."

"We weren't there to confiscate it," Cole said tightly. "We were confirming whether it was used in the commission of a crime. Another shooting."

"No," Rosa said, shaking her head. "He was getting out of the life. I know you think I'm lying, but he was. Until you came about the car, he was doing really good. And whoever it was you were asking about, the state employee who was shot at? He didn't know what you were talking about. I can tell when my brother is lying. He wasn't lying about that."

Cole and Luke shared a look. "Where is he now, Rosa?"

She shrugged. "I honestly don't know. Look, I knew he was going to try to escape. You're right. But I haven't seen him." She glanced at her sister. "And anyway, he wouldn't come here."

Her older sister nodded at them. "Rosa's right about that. He knows I'd turn him in."

"Where would he go?" Cole asked, even as a thousand curse words filled his mind. Maybe Dominic Elliard wasn't even who they were looking for.

"I don't know. He had some places, but they were in Kings territory. When he told Leonardo he wanted out, begged him for Ed Jr.'s sake, Leonardo was going to let him go. But it meant Dominic wasn't welcome there anymore. He wouldn't go there."

"Thanks for your time," Luke said, handing over his card. "Please call us if you think of anything else, or if you hear from Dominic."

Then he and Luke headed outside. After Rosa closed the door behind him, Cole looked at his partner. "What do you think?"

"I believe her. I don't think Dominic took Shaye."

"Then who did?"

"KEN TOBEK," SHAYE said softly, turning away from Dominic, gagged and tied up with rope, his head resting against his chest on the far side of the barn.

The flashlight slowly lowered, and her abductor smiled. "So, you *do* remember."

She was right.

Please, please understand my desperate attempt to leave a clue, Cole, she willed him. *Talk to your brother.*

Shaye blinked and blinked, until the spots in front of her eyes cleared and she could get a good look at Tobek. He'd aged a lot since she'd last seen him in that courtroom, but the easy-to-overlook exterior didn't hide the fury behind his eyes.

He was going to kill her. The knowledge

hit her instantly, with certainty, but instead of making her panic, a strange calm came over her.

There had to be a reason Tobek would bring her all the way out here, instead of pulling that car over as soon as they hit the boonies, shooting her and leaving her in a field. And there had to be a reason Elliard was here.

The voice in her head sounded like Cole, and Shaye glanced back at Elliard, suddenly realizing. "He's your patsy, isn't he? You're planning to frame my death on him?"

Tobek laughed, and it was part amused, part nasty. "Maybe. It was so easy. Once he shot up that police station, it was like he was handing me an out, even better than the alibi I'd cooked up. And especially after you got away from me that first time and I'd needed to set up another alibi. And then your boyfriend came to visit me… I knew I was right to have adjusted my original plan."

"You left the gun used to shoot at me at Roy's Grocery in Kings territory, then called in the anonymous tip," Shaye said, leaning her weight on her right foot. Her broken toes throbbed, sending pain all the way up to her hip, which seemed to remind her leg it had recently had a bullet in it, because that was throbbing now, too.

"You're smarter than you look," Tobek said, singsongy.

"Why?" Shaye asked. "You spent a month in jail. You can move on. Why come after me now, after all this time?"

"A month in jail?" he echoed. "Like that's no big deal?" His voice raised until he was yelling. "You told a courtroom full of people that I tried to kill my wife!"

He had. Shaye had no doubt about it. If Cole and Luke hadn't shown up at the Tobek residence when they had, Becca Tobek would be dead. Ken had only been convicted of assault, and shouldn't he feel lucky he'd gotten off so easy? Shouldn't he be moving on, thankful the justice system had gotten it wrong?

He shrugged, his voice going back to the odd monotone she'd heard in the courtroom a year ago, the monotone that had jiggled free a memory when he'd broken into Cole's house. "I can't let you get away with that. Besides…" He grinned, and it was scarier than his yelling. "You're only part of my plan."

Please, please don't go after Cole, Shaye thought, glancing around the barn again, wondering if there was anything she could get her hands on to use as a weapon. But it was hard to see well, just shafts of moonlight filtering down through the broken roof and Tobek's flashlight beam. There might have been a workbench behind Elliard, but that was way too far away to be useful to her.

"But this is all falling into place even better than I could have ever planned," Tobek continued, sounding gleeful. "Because Elliard over there is a violent, violent felon. A gang member. They're pretty indiscriminate about who they kill."

Shaye frowned. What was he talking about? Framing Elliard for her murder wouldn't look indiscriminate; Elliard had a known grudge. What was she missing?

"Now move," Tobek said, suddenly all business. He gestured with his gun toward Elliard, and when she glanced back, she saw something she'd missed before.

A second set of ropes beside Elliard.

Shaye put her hands up. "Ken—"

"Don't try to sweet-talk me." He made a disgusted noise. "Women. You're all the same. You think you can convince me this isn't all your fault? Not going to happen. Now move."

Breath caught in Shaye's throat as she realized the rest of Tobek's plan. "You're going to try to kill your wife again, aren't you?"

Tobek gave a forced laugh. "Not me. Elliard. And he's going to succeed. But you? You're feistier than you look." His gaze dropped over her, and her hands fell to her sides, yanking down her T-shirt as far as she could.

"It's true actually. I didn't expect you to knock out my taillight. I'm going to have to fix that. But Elliard didn't expect it, either." Tobek shrugged. "Because after he killed Becca, you almost got the upper hand. You actually managed to stab him before he shot you."

A jolt went through Shaye as he laid out his plan so casually. He was going to shoot her. Panic threatened at the instant reminder of how it had felt when the bullet had gone into her leg at Roy's Grocery.

Tobek shrugged again. "Too bad you both died from your wounds." He glanced around. "And by the time police found you way out here in Elliard's hiding spot, your bodies were in pretty bad shape. So, forensics aren't going to help you much this time, are they?"

He pointed at the ropes next to Elliard. "Now move. I've got to work in the morning."

Chapter Twenty

"I need updates now," Cole said as soon as Marcos picked up his call. "I'm not so sure Elliard is behind this anymore. We need a new lead."

Where was Shaye? *Hang on, honey,* he tried to will her.

"Okay," Marcos said, his voice all business, but Cole could tell anyway. There was nothing promising.

Cole's shoulders slumped, and Luke took his hand off the wheel for a second and clamped it on Cole's shoulder. "We'll find her," he mouthed as Marcos's voice came over the speaker again.

"The lab guys didn't find any prints besides yours and Shaye's in the bedroom or on the window."

"Not surprising. What about the neighbors? Did they hear anything? Did anyone see a car on the street that didn't belong? Maybe an old Taurus?"

"No. And no one was answering at Tobek's house, but officers paid his brother-in-law a visit. He said Tobek *has* borrowed his cars before, but that everything is in storage now."

"Cars?" Luke asked. "How many does he have?"

"Five. Two he keeps at the house and three at a garage he rents downtown."

"And Tobek has the keys?"

"Well, he's not supposed to, but the brother-in-law thinks he swiped a set of his keys."

"Is he sure everything is in storage?" Cole asked, as the new information made his detective's instinct buzz. He glanced at Luke. "But Tobek's alibi was good."

Luke nodded, and from the furrow between his eyebrows, Cole could tell he was having the same internal debate.

"As far as he knows, yeah."

"Get the plate numbers on them anyway," Luke suggested. "Put them out on the wire."

"Already did," Marcos replied. "I gave them to Hiroshi. He's on it. Meanwhile, we don't have any sightings of a car that fits the description from the shooting at Roy's Grocery. And so far, the Kings' hideouts you all know about are clean—well, empty. But they're still checking."

"What about Kings members? Any of them talking?" Luke asked.

"Just demanding lawyers. But Leonardo did say—hang on." There was some paper rustling; then Marcos continued, like he was reading from something he'd written down.

"Elliard is going to have some explaining to do. And if he thinks I don't know about his place in the country, he's wrong."

"What does that mean? We have an address?" Cole frowned over at Luke. Elliard had a place in the country?

"He's refusing to say any more, although officers did say they heard him muttering later about it being a stupid plan, how Dominic would never have the money or skills to build there anyway, so I don't know what kind of place it is. Your officers think he's keeping the location to himself, planning to go after Elliard when we let him go."

"Maybe we should let him go," Luke said.

"What?" Cole's and Marcos's voices overlapped.

"I know right now we don't think it's Elliard. But we still can't account for him, and the timing is suspicious. What if we let Leonardo go and follow him to Elliard's hiding spot?"

Cole's pulse picked up at the suggestion, and he nodded, liking the idea. "Except he's not likely to lead us right there. He's too smart to go right there."

"Unless we piss him off enough," Marcos suggested. "Make him believe Elliard was trying to pin the shooting on Leonardo by leaving the gun in his territory."

Cole frowned, shaking his head. "We got that anonymous call while Elliard was still in the hospital, under guard. If he made a call on a hospital phone, we could have traced it. It didn't come from there. It came from a burner phone."

"His sister visited," Luke said. "Maybe she brought him one. Do we have a better lead right now?"

"What about Shaye's coworkers?" Cole asked, still troubled by Rosa's certainty that her brother wasn't involved in Shaye's shooting.

"None of them thought Shaye had any enemies, and the only secret admirer they mentioned was you," Marcos said, a little amusement slipping into his tone at the end.

"Great," Cole muttered.

"But one of them did say something about a rusted-out Taurus they'd seen a few times parked on the street behind the lab."

"Away from the station," Luke said. "Where the cops would be less likely to see it."

"He did track her from the lab," Cole said. "So how did he follow her to my house? You think he followed me, and I didn't see him?" The idea made guilt join the fear and anger rolling in his gut.

"Let's just worry about finding her now," Luke said. "What's our next move?"

"I agree with Luke. Let's try letting Leonardo go—" Marcos started, but Cole cut him off as realization struck.

"Marcos, what did Shaye say to you last

night?" His heart rate started to pick up, knowing he was onto something.

"What do you mean?"

"You almost broke down the door. You said she sounded weird. What were her exact words, about the bed?" The comment he'd brushed off that had made no sense to him. Maybe it had been Shaye's way of sending him a message.

There was a long pause, and Cole knew his brother was trying to remember precisely.

"She said, 'Tell him I was right. His bed is more comfortable than mine.'"

"That's it," Cole said, his pulse skyrocketing.

"What?" Luke asked, giving him a confused glance as he continued to drive toward Rosa's house, where they'd originally talked to Elliard.

"Turn around," Cole said. "The part about the bed was just to make it sound like it wasn't a hint to her abductor. Shaye was telling me she was right. It was Ken Tobek."

"WAIT," SHAYE SAID, desperate to keep Tobek talking, to figure out a plan. Once she was tied up, her chances of survival—slim as they looked right now—dropped even lower.

"Come on now," Tobek said, wiggling the gun. "Don't make this difficult. Because I'm still willing to shoot you in the kneecaps if I have to, but that's going to make everything so messy."

"Look, I just—I deserve to know the rest of this. Come on. How do you think you're going to get away with killing your wife? You don't think the police will find that suspicious? That Elliard here broke out of the hospital just to kill me and your wife? How many times do you think you can pay your coworker to lie for you?"

Tobek frowned. "I didn't pay him. And believe me—he's not giving me up. Not unless he wants to go to jail himself."

"I'm sure the police would give him some leniency for helping—"

"Not that. He's doing me this little favor because I caught him with the boss's daughter after work one evening." Tobek laughed. "In the boss's office. And she's seventeen. Trust me. I told him all about how seventeen is still a child in the eyes of the law...and other prisoners. We all know what happens to child rapists in prison."

Shaye shook her head, trying not to look as disgusted—by both of them—as she felt. "I'm sure—"

"Oh, he believes me. Doesn't matter whether she's secretly dating him or not. The guy's a nervous nimrod. And anyway, I don't need an alibi for the middle of the night. I was at home asleep. Where else would I be?" He pointed the gun. "Now stop stalling, because I'm on a timeline here."

Shaye turned slowly, limping toward Elliard,

who still hadn't moved. Her breath caught. "Is he already dead?" she asked, not sure she wanted to know the answer.

"Nah, he's not dead. Trust me—I learned a thing or two from the last time. I'm going to be real careful, so everything lines up, just in case. Though I'm sure that by the time police find you, you'll be so decayed that figuring out exactly when you died will be a miracle."

Shaye shivered, trying not to imagine it but unable to help herself. She worked in a forensics lab. She'd seen those kinds of pictures. She clasped a hand to her heart. Cole would see those pictures of her. Tears pricked her eyes, knowing what it would do to him. He'd blame himself.

For all the times she'd accused him of not opening up to her, the truth was, she knew him better than she'd ever realized. Because she knew, without a doubt, that he'd never recover from this.

"You'd be surprised what we can do in that lab. For example, they're going to be able to tell that this whole thing is staged." She took a breath, leaning on all the knowledge she'd learned outside her own specialty over that year she'd spent in the lab.

"They'll recover the marks on Elliard's wrists showing he was tied up before he died. Those go deeper than you think. They'll reconstruct the scene, realize that the knife marks on him are too deep or the wrong angle or had to have been made by someone taller, heavier. My prints will be in the wrong place because I didn't actually hold it in the way you would if you were stabbing someone. The—"

"Stop it!" Tobek moved forward quickly, getting in her face and making her stumble backward.

She tripped, landing on her butt, her T-shirt riding up again. His gaze followed, and Shaye quickly yanked it down.

"I guess it's a good thing I kidnapped a forensics expert, then, isn't it?" Tobek said, leaning toward her.

If she'd been stronger—if her left leg wasn't in serious pain, her shoulders weak—she might have tried looping her legs around his, pulling him down when he was off balance. But she knew it was a losing move, and she wasn't quite at the point of trying something she knew had no chance of succeeding. Not yet. But she was quickly getting there.

"Because you're going to help me get it right," Tobek said.

"Why would I help you?" Shaye spat, trying to sound brave despite her terror. "You're going to kill me anyway. Shooting my kneecaps first isn't going to make me help you get away with it."

"Really?" Tobek grinned, and it was so full of menace and glee, she shrank into the ground a little. "Don't forget I know where your boyfriend lives. You do what I tell you, or when I'm finished here, I'm making a trip back to see him."

THE GARAGE DOOR rolled up at the storage unit with frustrating slowness.

Cole bent down, trying to see inside before it was finished opening.

"They're all here," the man standing between him and Luke said with exasperation.

And they were. Three cars, the rusty Taurus Cole couldn't believe was still running right in the middle.

"Now can I go back to bed?" Tobek's brother-in-law demanded.

They'd woken him in the middle of the night, pressuring him to drive with them out to the storage unit where he kept his extra cars. Cole had been so certain they'd find the Taurus missing—or possibly one of the other vehicles.

He looked at his partner. "What now?"

Luke's gaze was still on the brother-in-law. "Where might Ken go if he wasn't at home?"

"I don't know," the brother-in-law said. "Jeez. We're not even that close. Honestly, I only put up with him for my wife. The guy is kind of a tool."

"He doesn't own any other places? Doesn't go anywhere particular, like a hunting cabin or something?"

"No. Tobek doesn't hunt. He drinks. Look, I don't know what you suspect him of now—"

"What do you mean by *now*?" Cole asked.

Tobek's brother-in-law rolled his eyes. "He went to jail before for assaulting his wife. Poor Becca. Now her, I did like."

"Right. Okay, well—"

"I don't know where he'd go. Honest. And yeah, he's been a little, I don't know, moodier than usual lately, but I hardly think he's using my car to commit crimes."

"Well, we'd still like your permission for our lab to take a look at it," Luke said.

The man threw up his hands. "Fine. Can I go home and go back to bed now?"

"Yeah."

He yanked the door down, which closed a lot faster than it had opened, then stomped back to his vehicle, while Cole and Luke stood in the deserted storage area, staring at each other.

"Has anyone talked to Tobek's ex-wife?" Luke asked.

"Yeah. Hiroshi and Wes just called and woke her up a few minutes ago. I got the update on the drive here while you were riding with Tobek's brother-in-law. She says she hasn't heard from him since he got out of jail. But Hiroshi says it's pretty clear she's still scared of him."

"Okay. Well, let's check in with Marcos

again," Luke suggested, and Cole prayed his brother would have a new lead for them.

He dialed Marcos's cell, and his brother picked up before the first ring finished. "Any news?"

"I was hoping you'd have some," Marcos replied. "But look, I'm on my way to Tobek's house right now."

"What? Why?"

"Take me off speaker."

Cole glanced at Luke, who turned away, glancing around the storage unit, as Cole hit the speaker button and pressed the phone to his ear. "Okay, it's just us. What is it?"

"I know you wanted Hiroshi to go back and check the garage for Tobek's Benz, but I'm having him wait at the house instead. Hiroshi can't go inside the house without risking his job."

"I wasn't asking—"

"Yeah, but if you don't know anywhere else

he might be, we need to check. It would be stupid of him, but what if Shaye's in his house?"

Cole's hand clenched the phone too tight. "If she's in there, we go in with the cavalry."

"I hear you. I don't think she is, but we need to check."

"Hiroshi's not the only one who'd be risking his job doing that without a warrant," Cole warned, swearing inwardly. He should be there, doing what Marcos thought was his responsibility since Shaye had been taken while he was at the house.

"Don't worry," Marcos said, his tone upbeat. "I won't get caught. I'll call you back once I've cleared it."

"Be careful."

"What are you going to do?"

Cole glanced at Luke. "Right now the only move I can think of is the one we talked about earlier. Let Leonardo go, and see if he can lead us to Elliard."

Chapter Twenty-One

"I should have killed Becca first," Tobek muttered, gesturing with the gun and walking toward her so she scooted back until she bumped something.

Shaye turned around and realized it was the legs of a workbench. Why was it here in this old barn? She couldn't see what was on it from this angle, but she wondered if Tobek had left anything up there she could use as a weapon.

"It's going to mess up your plan of how this whole thing is going to be interpreted," Shaye said.

Tobek scowled at her. "I knew I should have

grabbed her first. But Elliard here just fell into my lap. I went to the hospital, hoping to snatch something of his I could leave at her house, and what did I find? This idiot sneaking out a service entrance." He kicked Elliard's leg with his shoe, then shrugged when Elliard didn't move.

"What's wrong with him?" Shaye asked.

"He didn't want to come with me. I had to use a little persuasion."

"What does that mean?"

Tobek stuck the gun in her face, inches from her nose, his face right behind it, breathing whiskey on her again. "It means I knocked him out. For a gang member, he's not so tough."

He'd also been recovering from a serious gunshot wound, Shaye wanted to say, but she didn't. She just nodded, then risked, "That will show up on an autopsy."

He gave her a mocking smile. "That's okay. *You* did that. Probably right before you stabbed him. The gun went off in the struggle and—

oops." Tobek shrugged. "You got hit and didn't survive."

Shaye shivered. This man was crazy. She'd known he was guilty when she'd taken the stand, known in her heart that if he wasn't convicted, he'd go after his wife again some-day—she'd even warned Becca Tobek of it when he'd been convicted of only assault. But she never expected he'd take such joy in the whole process, be willing to take out so many other people, too.

"All right, you've asked enough questions." He stood again, took a step back and leveled the gun on her. "Do I have to go and kill Becca first, then come back for you two?"

Shaye swallowed. The truth was he did. The medical examiner was good. And she didn't believe that she'd lie here rotting so long they wouldn't be able to tell. Cole would find her. In her heart she believed that. Whether it took days or weeks, he'd find her. And then the autopsy and the labs would show the truth. But Becca Tobek thought she was safe. It had been a year since she'd divorced Ken. She didn't have a detective watching over her.

As much as Shaye wanted Tobek to leave so she could try to escape, even if she managed to get free, she doubted she'd find help faster than Tobek could find and kill Becca. They were in the middle of nowhere. And it wasn't like she had a cell phone.

"No," she whispered, hoping she hadn't just signed her own death warrant.

"Good." He sounded gleeful. "Because I really want to save the best for last. No offense, but you're just the appetizer." His gaze dropped down her bare legs. "Although you're a tasty-looking appetizer."

Bile rose in Shaye's throat, and she tried to scoot backward more, but there was nowhere to go. Tobek was standing in front of her, slightly to her right, so she shifted left, bumping Elliard and making his head fall on her shoulder. She jumped, and Tobek laughed.

"Don't worry," he said, sounding slightly disappointed. "I'm not planning to leave my DNA on you." He glanced at his watch as Shaye felt something against her hip.

What was it? She leaned into Elliard a little more, realizing he had something hard in his jacket pocket. *A phone?* Her pulse jumped, and she wondered if she should backtrack on her claim that he didn't need to worry about the order of the deaths, but then she realized it wasn't a phone. It was too small for that.

"Time's wasting," Tobek said. "I have a lot to do tonight. We'd better get moving. So let's talk forensics."

Shaye nodded, only half paying attention to him now. Could it be possible? Did Elliard have a pocketknife that Tobek hadn't found?

It could make sense. Elliard had slipped away from his guard, gotten out of his cuffs. Someone could have helped him, brought him something to pick the lock with. A pocketknife had all kinds of tools in it. One of them might fit in the lock on a pair of handcuffs.

But how did she get it out of Elliard's pocket, open it and attack before Tobek shot her?

"SHAYE'S BEEN MISSING for hours." Cole knew he was stating the obvious, but he couldn't help it, just like he couldn't help the panic pressing down on his chest. "What if this is another dead end?"

"This is something proactive we can do now," Luke said. "Your brother is checking into Tobek at his house. You've got officers searching for any other places he could be. We're covering all our bases."

Cole knew his partner was right. They were doing everything they would be if this were any other kidnapping case. The problem was this wasn't any other kidnapping case. This was Shaye, the woman he wanted to spend the rest of his life with.

How had he been so blind about this? Everyone else had seen it. His brothers had been teasing him mercilessly about Shaye for two years, trying to get him to ask her out. Even Luke had joined in a time or two. They'd all known what he'd been trying to deny. His feelings for her weren't a solid friendship mixed with a too-strong attraction. They were flat-out love. And now he might never get to tell her.

"You'll get the chance to tell her how you feel," Luke said, and, for a second, Cole thought he'd spoken the words out loud.

Then he realized Luke just knew him that well. "I messed up," he told his partner.

"Well, let's see if he can help us remedy things," Luke replied, nodding toward the front of the station, where the head of the Kings was sauntering down the steps.

"Looks like they did a good job of making Leonardo think he was intimidating them enough to let him go," Cole said. He could practically see Leonardo's smirk from here.

"Yeah." Luke slouched low in his seat, even though they were parked out in the street, far enough away that Leonardo would have a hard time seeing them.

Cole did the same, watching over the edge of the dashboard. "Please, please go straight to Elliard's hiding place," Cole willed him.

Leonardo did a mock salute to the officers who'd walked out behind him, then climbed into a car someone had dropped off for him and revved the engine. He spun the wheels, leaving behind a plume of smoke as he gunned it out of the station parking lot.

"This is going to be interesting," Luke said, flipping on the headlights, switching into Drive and following.

Luckily, even this late at night, there was some traffic. When Leonardo hopped onto the freeway, Luke visibly relaxed and dropped back a few more car lengths.

"Where's he going?" Cole wondered aloud ten minutes later.

"Leonardo did say Elliard's secret hiding place was somewhere in the country," Luke reminded him just as Cole's phone rang.

"Marcos," Cole answered, putting the call on speaker. "What did you find?"

"No sign of Tobek," his brother said. "His Benz isn't here, either. But I had Hiroshi put it out and we actually got a hit. Patrol officers driving by the storage place you visited earlier spotted it parked nearby."

Luke glanced at the phone, frowning. "But his brother-in-law said he wasn't missing any cars. And the right number of vehicles were there."

"What if he stole someone else's?" Cole asked. "A lot of people store their summer vehicles there, stuff they don't drive when it gets cold. He could easily figure someone wouldn't miss it for the night, return it before morning." As he said the words, he recognized the truth in them, but also what that meant for Shaye.

Dawn was coming fast now. If Tobek's plan was to be back home by morning, Shaye didn't have much time left.

"We need to get the manager there, see if any units have been tampered with," Cole said.

"What about security?" Luke asked. "Wouldn't they have noticed if someone drove out of there with a car?"

"Not if they expected him," Cole said. "Tobek has been there before. He could have gone in with his brother-in-law's key, then driven out with a different car. The security guys probably don't match vehicles to people, just access."

"But then his name will show up on a log," Luke said.

"Yeah, but that doesn't mean much if we

can't tie him to a crime. He probably wasn't too worried about that."

"I'm on it," Marcos said. "I'll call security and find out what car he drove out of there, then get them to figure out whose it was and run license plates so we can put a BOLO on it."

By then, would it be way too late?

"He's getting off," Luke said, drawing Cole's attention back to Leonardo, who was indeed taking the exit ahead of them.

"That doesn't lead anywhere. It's all farm-land," Cole said.

"Exactly," Luke agreed.

"Marcos, I'm going to have to call you back. But let me know the second you have something. We'll let you know if we need backup."

"Be careful."

"I will," Cole promised, his fists opening and closing on his lap. He didn't plan to need backup. Wherever Leonardo was leading them, if Shaye was there, Cole planned to take Elliard down with his bare hands if he had to.

"He's slowing down," Luke said, swearing and dropping way back.

Cole prayed the Kings' leader was so focused on his mission, he wasn't bothering to check his rearview mirror. Because if he did, there'd be no missing them.

There was no way for Luke to stay far enough back not to be seen, not out here in the middle of nowhere.

"There aren't even any houses here," Luke said. "I think he might have made us. He could be leading us on a wild-goose chase."

"What's that?" Cole asked as Leonardo suddenly pulled off the road.

Luke slowed the car down some more. "Looks like a barn? But I don't see anything else. Do you think this is some kind of trap?" He reached for his phone. "Maybe we should call for backup."

Cole yanked a pair of binoculars out of the

glove compartment and focused them on Leonardo as he climbed out of the car, parked down a little path from the barn. "There's another car there, sort of hidden in those bushes."

"This could definitely be an ambush."

"No, I don't think so." Cole's pulse picked up as Leonardo lifted his trunk and pulled out a shotgun. "Not for us anyway. He's got a shotgun."

Leonardo slammed the trunk and started walking toward the barn.

"This is it!" Cole said. "This must be Elliard's place. Shaye could be in there. Go!"

Luke hit the gas, and Cole's head slammed back against his seat as he wrestled for the pistol in his holster.

Ahead of them, Leonardo glanced back, spotted them and then started running for the barn.

IT WAS NOW or never, Shaye thought as Tobek stuffed the gun in the back of his waistband

and bent down, wrapping the rope around her wrists.

"Ouch," she yelped. "Remember what I said about the ropes leaving marks?"

He squinted at her, like he wasn't sure if she was helping him to avoid being shot in the kneecaps or trying to play him for a fool.

She tried to look innocent, sure she just looked terrified.

Tobek grunted at her, easing up on the rope, and Shaye braced herself, getting ready to leap for Elliard, praying what was in his pocket was what she thought it was.

Before she could act, Elliard let out a low moan; then his head rolled back before he straightened it. He glanced around as Tobek leaped away from her, reaching for his gun.

Now or never, Shaye reminded herself, and she shoved her hands into Elliard's pocket.

Then he was squirming, spitting the gag

out of his mouth, yanking at his ropes, pushing at her.

Shaye got her hands free as Tobek frantically tried to bring his gun back around. He
dropped it when Elliard let out a huge roar of
pain or anger and heaved himself to his feet.

As Tobek dived for his gun, Shaye glanced
down at the object in her hand. She was right!
Panicked, she fumbled to open the pocketknife and get to her feet as Tobek got his hands
around the gun and Elliard launched himself
at Tobek.

A gunshot blasted, and Shaye flinched but
managed to open the knife. It was tiny, and the
idea of bringing a knife to a gunfight hit her
hard. She glanced at Elliard, sure he'd been
shot, but he hadn't realized his feet were bound
and he'd tripped. Tobek's shot had gone wide,
but he was aiming again, swinging the gun
back at Elliard.

Shaye rushed forward, unable to believe she

was risking her life for a gangster. She led with the knife, hoping to reach Tobek before he could readjust.

His gaze jumped to her; then his gun swung for her, but Elliard got to his knees, batting Tobek's hand aside with his bound ones and sending the gun flying.

Tobek responded with an uppercut, and Elliard flew backward, smacking his head on the workbench legs.

Shaye jabbed, but somehow Tobek grabbed her wrist, twisting until she dropped the knife, yelping at the pain. He took a swing at her, and she jerked out of the way, falling to her side.

Then he was moving toward her, holding the pocketknife she'd dropped in one hand and the knife he'd pressed to her throat in Cole's house in the other. She didn't know where he'd had it, but he was grinning, something pure evil in his eyes, as she shoved herself back to her feet.

She moved away from him, her hands up, reminding him, "This will never pass for a fight between me and Elliard." Her back bumped the workbench and then there was nowhere else to go.

COLE LEAPED OUT of the car before Luke even had it in Park. "Get the shotgun from the trunk," Cole yelled at his partner as he cleared his pistol from his holster and ran after Leonardo.

Leonardo swung around and fired. Cole ducked, wasting precious seconds glancing at Luke, but his partner's head popped back up over the steering wheel and he gave a thumbs-up.

Then Leonardo was racing for the barn again, and Cole hurried after him, even as a gunshot fired inside the structure—this one from a pistol. Fear spiked in Cole's veins, and he prayed he hadn't found Shaye only to have her killed seconds before he made it to her side.

"Stop!" Cole screamed, but Leonardo ignored him, darting inside the barn.

Cole pushed his strides, going as fast as he could, and skidding to a stop when he made it through the doors.

In front of him, Leonardo was lifting his shotgun to fire again. He was aiming at Elliard, who was groaning on the ground, but then Tobek spun toward him, dropped to the ground and grabbed a pistol. Leonardo moved the shotgun toward him.

Behind Tobek was Shaye, her hands up, backed against a workbench. She was *directly* behind Tobek. A blast from a shotgun could go through Tobek and into Shaye.

Tobek lifted his pistol, and Cole lined up his weapon as Leonardo's finger started to drop under the trigger guard.

It felt like it was all happening in slow motion and Cole could see it all playing out in his head. Luke was coming, but he wouldn't get here with the shotgun before three bullets were fired. Cole was going for Leonardo, but Tobek saw what he was doing and was starting to shift his weapon toward Cole.

Cole clenched his teeth. If he could stop Leonardo, Tobek could shoot him. Cole knew his partner would get in there and take out Tobek before he could kill Shaye. And that was all that mattered.

Time sped up again, as Cole heard himself screaming, saw Shaye twisting backward and saw Tobek snarling. Cole pulled the trigger, and Leonardo dropped, falling on top of his shotgun milliseconds before his finger cleared the guard and a shot went off.

Cole turned to Tobek, even though he knew he wouldn't make it.

Tobek knew it, too. He was actually grinning as his finger started to press the trigger. Then his eyes widened, and he crumpled.

Behind him Shaye was breathing heavily,

holding what looked like a metal C-clamp in her hand that she'd grabbed off the workbench and slammed into Tobek's head.

"Shaye," Cole breathed. She was alive. He'd made it in time. His vision blurred, and Cole realized tears of relief had clouded his eyes. He blinked them back, and then she was limping toward him, still holding that C-clamp.

"Seriously? I missed it?"

Cole turned and Luke was in the doorway, brandishing the shotgun. "We could have used that a second ago," he teased his partner. "But luckily Shaye's got good aim, too."

Luke's gaze dropped to her makeshift weapon and he nodded, setting down the shotgun and pulling out his cuffs. He checked Leonardo's pulse, then shook his head and moved on to Tobek as Cole covered him with his pistol and Shaye kept coming toward him.

"Out cold," Luke said after checking Tobek. He cuffed the guy anyway, adding, "Nice job,

Shaye." Then he checked Elliard, stood up and shook his head. "He's passed out, too. I'll call for reinforcements to transport these two back to the station and the coroner for Leonardo."

"Thanks," Cole told his partner, holstering his weapon and striding toward Shaye, who fell forward, letting him catch her. "Are you okay?"

She smiled shakily up at him. "Some cuts and bruises. A couple of nicks from that knife, and some broken toes. I'll live." Her smile shifted, changing into something serious. "I knew you'd find me. I'm so glad you found me before—"

"Me, too," Cole said, not wanting to think about the alternative. He bent, then carefully scooped her into his arms. "Shaye, I don't know what I would have done—"

She pressed a finger to his lips. "I'm okay." She gave him another trembling smile. "And now we can think about getting back to what we started before you got that darn call about Elliard."

Had that been today? It felt like a lifetime ago.

And speaking of a lifetime…

Cole kissed her hand, then kissed her lips, then spoke fast before he lost his nerve and waited until they were somewhere besides a barn in the middle of nowhere with his partner keeping watch over three violent criminals, two wounded and one dead. It wasn't the most romantic spot in the world, but he didn't want to wait another minute to tell Shaye how he felt.

"I do want to get back to that. I want to get back to dating you, and I want to work every day to deserve you. I want you to move in with me." When she opened her mouth, he hurried on quickly. "Or I can move in with you. I want to marry you and have babies together and live a long, happy life together."

Shaye's eyes widened, her lips moving but no words coming out. Then she laughed shakily. "Cole, we've barely started dating yet."

"I know. And I know it's fast, but—"

"But I like that plan," she cut him off. "Let's take it one step at a time. Because I love you. And I want that future with you."

He smiled at her, and he could tell by the way she was looking up at him that what he was thinking was plain on his face. But he said it anyway, because she deserved to hear it. "I love you, too, Shaye. Now let's get out of here."

He glanced back at Luke. "You got this?"

"Cavalry is on the way," Luke said, giving him a thumbs-up. "Keys are in the car."

"Good." Cole shifted Shaye in his arms and started walking. "Because I'm ready to start that future right now."

Epilogue

What did the chief of police want?

Shaye straightened her blouse and shoved down her nerves as she crossed the parking lot from the forensics lab to the police station. Funny how the walk didn't seem so scary anymore. But getting called to the chief of police's office? A little nerve-racking.

It had been three weeks since Tobek had taken her hostage in that barn. And while she'd wanted to drive out of there and straight back to Cole's house, he'd taken her to the hospital instead. They'd taped up her toes, inspected her cuts and told her to take it easy. By the time they were back in the car, her adrenaline had faded and she'd fallen asleep.

She'd woken to him carrying her inside his house, then he'd helped her clean up in the shower and tucked her into bed. The next morning, she'd learned Tobek and Elliard had been processed and were both heading to jail. She was dreading Tobek's trial, but Cole had assured her there was no way he was ever getting out again.

Since then things had fallen into a rhythm with Cole, like they'd been dating for years instead of weeks. She still had to pinch herself thinking about the things he'd said in that barn about their future. It wasn't that long ago she'd been daydreaming about him, thinking it would never be real.

Pulling open the door to the station, Shaye had a sudden flashback to the first day she'd arrived on the job and mistaken this building for the one she'd be reporting to. A smile quirked her lips, remembering how she'd turned a corner and slammed right into Cole. She'd stared up at him, turning beet red, knowing even then he was her fantasy man. And the reality was so much better than anything she could have imagined.

Confidence picked up her steps as she headed for that same turn she'd taken two years ago toward the chief's office. The hallway was emptier than usual, and Shaye wondered for an instant where everyone was. Then she rounded the corner and stopped in her tracks.

The hallway was filled with officers, and they were all staring at her. And was that… Shaye squinted through the crowd. It was. Andre and Marcos were here. What was going on?

She glanced around, looking for Cole, and then the crowd parted a little and he was walking through it. He strode up to her, then dropped to one knee, and her hands clasped over her mouth, smothering her gasp.

His hands were shaking a little as he opened a box, revealing a ring that seemed to catch the light from every angle. "Shaye, two years ago, right on this very spot, you changed my entire world. I didn't know it then, not really, though I probably should have, because you were on my mind every moment from then on."

"Cole," she whispered, dropping her hands from her lips. Her heart was thundering in her eardrums, and if it could burst from happiness, she was in some serious danger right now.

"I know being married to a cop might not be what you had in mind for your future, but—"

She dropped to her knees, too, taking his hands in hers, that gorgeous ring in the middle. "Oh, but it is. I'll tell you what. You teach me how to handle the worry that comes along with being married to a guy who runs into danger all the time, and I'll teach you how to open up more and value in yourself all the things I love about you. Deal?"

He grinned back at her. "Is that your way of saying yes?"

A smile trembled on her lips in response. "Did you ask me a question?" she teased.

He got serious, and, wow, did she love serious Cole, with his sky blue eyes laser focused on her. "Shaye Mallory, I'm looking for something a little different in my life."

The smile burst free as she remembered how not that long ago, he'd thought their differences would keep them apart. But the truth was she knew their differences would keep them going, make them stronger together.

"Will you marry me?"

"Yes," she whispered. "Oh, yes."

"We can't hear you!" someone called from the crowd. She was pretty sure it was Marcos.

Cole grinned as he slipped the ring on her finger and she yelled out, "Yes!"

Then the entire police station burst into applause, and Cole pulled her into his arms, kissing her the way he did in all her dreams. The way he was going to do for the rest of her life.

* * * * *